FOX & BROW
Copyri
Liberty Ja

The right of Liberty Jane Brown
work has been asserted by her in accordance with the Copyright,
Design, and Patents Act, 1988. All rights Reserved.

No reproduction, copy, or transmission of this publication may be
made without written permission. No paragraph of this publication
may be reproduced, copied, or transmitted save with the written
permission, or in accordance with the provisions of Copyright Act,
1956 (as amended). Any person who commits any unauthorised act in
relation to this publication may be liable to criminal prosecution and
civil claims for damages.

A CIP catalogue recording for this title is available from the British
Library.

ISBN 9798336243352

Fox & Brown Publishers
Harrogate, England
www.foxandbrownpublishing.co.uk

First Published 2024
Printed and bound in Great Britain

'Liberty Jane'
L.J. Brown

Based on a True Story

Dedications

For My Beautiful Friend & Editor

Not once have you let me down on this journey. You've listened to my crazy ideas and worked hard with me to get these books finished. You never gave up and always had vision. I don't think I could've done this without your guidance and love.

For My Senior Editor

You were the turning point in my career, and it was wonderful to meet you in Alabama, USA. I've learned so much from you, and now know how to write well, thanks to you. I'm forever in debt to your kindness and enthusiasm for me as a writer. I'll always now write a book as if it should be a movie!

Contents

Preface: Return to Innocence — 1

Chapter One: Smells Like Teen Spirit — 10
Chapter Two: Problem — 18
Chapter Three: Freedom — 24
Chapter Four: Unstoppable — 31
Chapter Five: Starving — 37
Chapter Six: Help! — 43
Chapter Seven: Bang a Gong (Get it on) — 52
Chapter Eight: Teardrops from My Eyes — 57
Chapter Nine: Cry to Me — 62
Chapter Ten: Castles Made of Sand — 79
Chapter Eleven: Stood Up — 86
Chapter Twelve: In My Mind — 95
Chapter Thirteen: Back to Black — 104
Chapter Fourteen: My Funny Valentine — 118
Chapter Fifteen: Trapped — 130
Chapter Sixteen: Stayin' Alive — 138
Chapter Seventeen: Pink Shoelaces — 144
Chapter Eighteen: 9PM (Till I Come) — 150
Chapter Nineteen: Stuck on a Feeling — 156
Chapter Twenty: Train Wreck — 163
Chapter Twenty-one: You'll Never Walk Alone — 168
Chapter Twenty-two: Around the World — 176

Chapter Twenty-three: Say My Name	184
Chapter Twenty-four: War Pigs	190
Chapter Twenty-five: Bad Ass Motherf*cker	196
Chapter Twenty-six: Don't Know Much	209
Chapter Twenty-seven: Tennessee Whisky	222
Chapter Twenty-eight: Born to be Wild	228
Chapter Twenty-nine: Everything I do	230

PREFACE

"Return to Innocence" ~ Enigma

"L.J., I'm interested—what were you like as a child? Has this gift always been with you?" he asked in a deep Alabama accent, amazed by me across the American diner. I looked into space and fell into deep thought.

1985

Dressed in my favourite blue dungarees, lying on my front with legs raised in the air, in my grandma's garden. Paper and crayons were spread all over a large sheet on the grass. My dolls were lined up facing me, and I was drawing and chatting away to them as if they were alive and interacting with me. I would talk for hours, showing them the pictures I had drawn and telling them stories I would make up.

I was full of wonder and adventure, fearing nothing. Life was simple and the world was full of magic.

There was a small hole in the fence of the garden that I could just about fit through. This led to a field filled with overgrown weeds. I snuck through, taking a handful of paper and a crayon and one of my dolls. Walking through the field, I looked up at the sky and watched the clouds moving slowly. Mouth wide open, I would try to figure out what the clouds resembled.

"Look, Dollyanna, it's a dragon with two heads! He hasn't seen us yet, but we better hide." I ducked down in the long grass, putting my finger to my lips to tell my doll to shush, and that we were playing hide-

and-seek until the cloud blew away. Pushing the weeds aside, I waded through the tall grass until I came to a clearing. There was an animal chewing grass—one I'd not seen before. I put my doll down and stood watching it. I moved forward and it jolted and moved away, then stopped and looked right at me.
It had big brown eyes, antlers pointing to the sky, and a big wet nose. It looked at me like it knew me. I didn't feel scared; I felt curious.

"Are you one of Santa Claus's reindeer?" I said softly. "It's nice to meet you. Why are you all alone?" There was a long pause as we just looked at each other. It was like time had stopped, it was so beautiful I didn't think anything, I just looked at the creature. "Are you hungry, Mr. Reindeer? You can have one of my crayons if you like—the pink one tastes of strawberries, but you will have to brush your teeth afterwards." I held out my hand to offer it to the animal. It continued to stare at me. "What about some nice fresh dandelions?" I pulled the weeds out of the earth and offered them to the delicate beast. It slowly moved forward, apprehensive, taking the smallest steps towards me. It stood in front of me. It was almost the same height as me. It tilted its head then took the weeds from my hand.

"You don't smell like Christmas, and your nose is wet. That tickles!" I giggled as the animal stepped back and ran away. It stopped to look back at me as if it were saying goodbye, then disappeared.

"Goodbye, it was nice to meet you! Tell Santa Claus I've been good!" I picked my doll up and spun around in a circle until I made myself dizzy and fell on my bottom in the grass.

I looked all around me. I could no longer see my grandma's house. Everything around me seemed so vast and big. The breeze blew through my hair, and all I could hear were busy bees, the wind rustling through the trees, and grass blowing in the breeze. Birds chirped. It was so peaceful and calm.

I took the scrunched-up paper out of my pocket and straightened it out, then began to write with my red crayon.

"Once upon a time, there was a little girl, and all she wanted to do was play with her dolls and draw pictures. One day, she sent a handsome prince one of her stories, and he sent one back asking her to marry him. The end." Feeling very proud of my story, I folded the paper into a paper airplane and threw it into the air. It didn't go very far, so I picked it up and held it in my hand, running through the grass making airplane noises.

The sun was shining on me, and I felt the warmth of its rays as I played, feeling so imaginative and alive. I ran up a steep hill to the top and let go of the paper from my hand, setting it free, watching in amazement and awe.

"Fly, paper airplane, fly high in the sky with the birds and the clouds. Send this to my prince so I can be a princess and live in a castle made of paper and I can write and draw all day long." A gust of wind took it. It flew and spun and spiralled until it was out of sight. I rolled down the hill in the grass, with no care in the world.

"L.J., sweetheart, where are you? It's teatime." A familiar, loving voice came from the distance. I stopped what I was doing to listen.

"I'm coming, Nanna!" I shouted back, looking for my doll, and followed the smell of her cooking all the way back.

I blinked as the waiter offered me more coffee."L.J., are you okay?"

Mike looked at me, concerned, my focus returned to the meeting.

"Oh, I'm sorry, I had a little flashback. In answer to your question, yes, I think being creative, being a writer, has perhaps always been with me." I smiled and nodded to the waiter for a top-up of coffee, my heart full of love for remembering who I was right at the start of my journey, and how beautiful my soul had always been, I'd just forgotten who I was…

"So do you think my book is good enough to make into a movie?" I turned my attention back to him, but I couldn't help feeling what I had just remembered.

"It's a box office hit already L.J., all that's left is to write the screenplay."

New York City. June 2023

Dressed immaculately in a black pinstriped suit and black stiletto heels, I was dressed to make an impression. I had a small silver brooch of a paper airplane that I had been gifted many years ago, attached to my jacket. I rubbed it for luck.

It was as if all my synapses had been hit with an overwhelming, disparate version of the world I'd known. I felt as though I'd been placed on a new planet. My eyes had never been as wide, and my heart had never pounded with such an unfamiliar rhythm, dazzled by its enchantment and wonder.

Look up, look left, look right – straight ahead was never-ending. The vast sprawl of the metropolis was surreal, like a glass Lego set, with the most beautiful lights, smells and sounds. I couldn't comprehend the explosion of feelings it set off in my mind, even though I was walking around it, like a tiny ant in a giant kingdom. Coming from the sleepy, quiet, peaceful landscape of the Yorkshire Dales, the most profound size comparison my mind could make was Ben Nevis, and that was now so small to me. A dot. New York was a million times the size of everything I'd ever seen back home. Then there were the endless honks of horns from yellow cabs, police sirens and fire trucks, impatiently rushing through the network of streets. On every corner someone selling something, donut stands everywhere, and the air filled with the smell of freshly brewed coffee. Twenty-four hours a day, this magic playground truly never slept.

I inhaled deeply waiting at a crosswalk, then walked across the road and towards the building. I had arrived at the New York Times. I was finally here. I couldn't feel my feet; it was like I was floating on a cloud, and the breeze was pushing me forward. I stared at the building, my mouth wide open. I blew my hair away from my face and gulped.

"Don't fuck this up, L.J." I said to myself, still in disbelief I had been given this incredible opportunity.

"Good morning." Two men dressed in smart suits opened the doors for me; I smiled and thanked them as I glided in, I was now in character. I explained my appointment and I was directed to reception, where a smart man dressed in a slightly too tight blue suit asked my name and showed me to the seating area where I sat inwardly nervous, outwardly a picture of strength and confidence.

I waited for what seemed forever, then my name was called. I stood up too fast, making my head spin, whilst trying to balance on my high heels and compose myself gracefully.

"Hello there, you must be L.J. I'm thrilled to have you today. My name's Adam, I'm one of the reporters here. I will be doing today's interview," he said, before turning on his heel and leading me towards a lift, flashing a smile of brilliant white teeth. We got into the lift, and he selected the top floor.

"How was your journey to New York, did you fly first class?"

"Standard, I'm afraid. I flew first class when I went to Alabama and there's a big difference. But it was fun, and I met some interesting people, even got a bit drunk." I giggled at the memory and how fast time had flown, drinking with strangers.

"Well, I hope you've had a lot of coffee today because this meeting is going to be quite intense. I have a lot of questions to ask you." He looked me up and down and then into my eyes. "You remind me of Daphne from Frasier with that accent." He smiled and looked to the floor, shifting his feet from side to side; the eye contact had seemingly embarrassed him slightly.

"In Alabama I was told I sounded like Mary Poppins. Feed the birds, tuppence a bag," I began singing. We both looked at each other and started to giggle; this was a great icebreaker.

The lift arrived at its destination and the doors opened. I was led to a large meeting room looking out over New York City, when imposter syndrome suddenly hit me.

Would you like a drink of water, iced tea?"

"Do you have anything stronger?" I joked, breaking the ice for a second time.

"Firstly, thank you for flying to New York to meet with me. It's a long way to come for one meeting!" he said assertively.

"I love America", I replied."And besides, I wanted to meet face-to-face – online meetings are not for me, the passion is lost by technology."

"It's a very interesting story, L.J.," he continued,"and from reading your books I know you've been on quite the adventure." his eyes looked at me curiously."L.J., the whole world knows about Pam and Tommy's sex tape, and Fifty Shades grossed $570 million at the global box office. How is your story going to beat that kind of exposure, when you don't even have a best-seller yet?"

I slowly stood up and walked towards the window, gazing out at New York City taking it all in my stride, then turned back to my interviewer.

"Because I have a story that will touch people's hearts, set them on fire and make them fall in love with themselves and life." I loved it he did not have a clue what was about to unfold.

The room fell silent. He cleared his throat."I'm sorry, do I have the right author? Your books, all your material, are about 7 years' worth of accounts of your true sexual experiences? A graphic account, I might add."

"No, that's what you think you read!" I walked around the boardroom table, picked up the books and walked to a nearby bin, throwing the books into it one by one.

"Are you serious?" His mouth was wide open.

I just flew across the pond for a two-hour meeting, I think you could consider that pretty serious, yes." I smiled at him professionally. "Adam, that's your name, right?" I'd researched every reporter at The Times before I got here.

"You were the only one equipped for the job, only your photo needs updating – I hardly recognised you." I had to do a bit of thinking on my feet. I drank some water and waited for his reply. He smiled showing his perfect white teeth, pursed his lips together and shook his head.

What makes me the best person to write L.J. Brown's exclusive, then?" He didn't break eye contact and his smile was filled with warmth.

You write with passion. When I read your work, it's not to sell a story, it's because you believe in your work, and it comes across that you tell the truth and don't make up lies. No one else at The Times, I believe, would understand my story, they would twist and distort and exaggerate my experience without seeing the real me or meaning of my journey." I shrugged my shoulders and sat back down at the table, now showing some vulnerability.

"I'm about to tell you the truth about me, the person behind the books. It's a very personal thing to share with anyone, let alone the entire world, America. I have been on an incredible journey, it's not just about sex." I searched his eyes for confirmation that he had understood the task in hand. He looked at me more seriously now, knowing that he was about to experience something he had not anticipated earlier that day in the lift. He then broke the silence and reached for the recording device next to him on the table.

It's the 21st of June 2023 at 11.11am. Location, The New York Times, interviewing Liberty Jane Brown for a world exclusive. Are you ready,

Miss Brown?" He looked at me mystifyingly.

Yes, I'm ready." I took a deep breath and gazed out of the window at the skyscrapers surrounding the building, the side of my face cold from the glass against it.

It all started in 1994, in Yorkshire, England, and I would have been about 14 years old.

CHAPTER ONE
NORTH YORKSHIRE, ENGLAND (1994)

"Smells Like Teen Spirit" ~ Nirvana

"L.J., as a special treat, you can eat in the front room today, since we have visitors," my mother shouted from the kitchen."Please go and wash your hands," she continued. I got up, nodded, and did as I was told. I walked past my mother to the sink and the smell of food hit my nostrils. I felt instantly sick.

My stepdad's mother was visiting and sharing a room with me, which I always hated. What I hated more, though, was her cooking. Her portions of food were massive, and until now I'd always had to stay at the table and eat every last scrap from my plate.

I watched as my grandmother served meat and potato pie with a mountain of mushy peas and mint sauce. I hated mushy peas. I looked at my mother with worried eyes, then took my tray and walked back into the living room to sit down and eat.

The front room was very small. It had a two-seater blue velvet sofa, two chairs, and a TV, which all the furniture faced, apart from the seat nearest the window where we had a plant that was in serious need of watering. The familiar music of the popular darts-themed TV quiz Bullseye was playing, introducing the show before it started. Bully the bull, animated in his red and white striped top, was driving the bus filled with contestants, before flying around the dartboard and introducing the host, Jim Bowen.

I stared at the TV as I pushed the food around my plate trying to separate the peas. "Sport please, Jim," said one of the contestants. My fork scraped loudly on the bottom of the plate, and everyone in the room turned to me, screwing their faces up. I put some pie on my fork and slowly put it in my mouth, closing my eyes as if I were in extreme pain. It tasted revolting, and I felt dizzy and nauseated.

"What's wrong with your food?" My stepfather stopped eating, banged his knife and fork down on his tray, and gritted his teeth at me.

"I… I… I don't like it," I stammered honestly, terrified of him.

"I go out to work every day to pay for that food on your plate, now EAT IT. Don't get up out of your seat until it's all gone." He looked at me with blazing angry eyes, then turned back to the TV.

Silent tears fell down my face as I put food into my mouth; then I involuntarily gagged and spat it back out onto my plate. My stepdad turned to me, his face boiling with anger. "You ungrateful spoilt little BRAT!" He stood up with his tray and placed it on his chair. As I was seated, he looked like a giant to me and I began to shake, looking at my mother for help. "This food not good enough for you? Think you're a princess, do you?"

"No, Daddy, I'm sorry, I just don't like it; it's making me feel sick." My heart was pounding in my chest and tears poured down my face as he continued to intimidate me.

"Your grandma cooked you this." He turned to her to make me feel ashamed, and she shook her head.

"If the girl doesn't want it, leave her be." She smiled at me, and I felt relief.

"Eat your food!" He bent over me, then lifted my plate, pushing the contents of the hot food onto my face, instantly scolding me. I felt the food drip off my face and onto my clothes. I couldn't see, I couldn't breathe, and I couldn't speak.

"Run. Run, L.J., run out of here," I heard a voice in my head.

"Bullseye," he shouted out, laughing at what he'd done, showing no remorse.

"WHAT ARE YOU DOING?" his mother screamed out, followed by my mother screaming,"She's just a girl. How could you?" She started to wail with tears, hitting him in the chest repeatedly. The screaming and shouting came from everywhere; agonising emotion filled the room. I wiped the food away from my eyes, and like a bullet I launched myself across the room, the food covering me and the floor as I ran. I reached for the door handle and didn't look back. I ran down the street as fast as I could with no shoes on. The floor was cold, and the stones were uncomfortable, but the pain in my face was now more apparent, burning as the cold air hit it.

The only place I could think of hiding where they couldn't find me was the den. It was an old hollow tree I'd found in the woods, not too far from my house, and only a child could fit inside. Some select members of the gang knew where it was; we kept cigarettes and cooking matches there so our parents wouldn't find them on us at home—it was the perfect hideout. I kept my notebook there for writing stories and a torch in case I ever had to stay the night. There was an emergency blanket too, half eaten by bugs.

I gently wiped the food off my face with the edge of the blanket, trying hard to catch my breath from crying. I hyperventilated, still in complete shock and terror. Going dizzy and shaking, I curled up into a ball and sobbed quietly.

"God, I will do anything, I promise I will be the best person on the planet for you if you could just make him go away from me and Mummy," I prayed. After some time, my breathing returned to normal, and I sat up and reached for a Lambert and Butler, which was neatly wrapped up in a paper towel I'd stolen from school. I struck a long cooking match and lit the cigarette, my hands still shaking.

Leaving the cigarette in my mouth, I turned to a plastic, double-wrapped bag, and pulled out my notebook filled with short stories. The pen was still stuck in the page from last time I'd opened it. I stared at the blank page, inhaled smoke, then coughed and went dizzy from the tobacco rush.

"Once upon a time, there was a girl who lived in a house with her stepdad. He was a complete and utter evil bastard," I said under my breath, looking around to check no one had found me. I continued to smoke one after the other as I wrote about my experience, changing his character into a big fat ugly giant. It helped me; it always did. When I wrote, I felt safe, and I had no one else to talk to about what was going on. Pages and pens became my best friends; they were always there, and I could tell them absolutely anything.

After a short time, I heard whistling and shouting in the distance; adults called out my name over and over again. I panicked and tried to calm myself so they wouldn't find me. I was not going back, not after this. Finally, other adults had seen what happened. He'd always been good at hiding and covering up what he did to me before.
"L.J., come home. The police are looking for you!" A desperate cry from my mother in the distance broke my heart. It wasn't her fault,

but she should have picked a more suitable father for me after Dad left. The voices continued for what seemed forever, then faded and went quiet. I sat up and peeped out of the tree to check if I could see anyone. The coast seemed to be clear, so I reached for another cigarette and took one out. My hand shook, my body now freezing cold, and the blanket damp. I looked at my muddy feet as I flicked ash onto the floor and brushed off some dirt.

I heard a twig snap in the distance. Quickly stubbing the cigarette out and getting back inside the tree, I froze to the spot in terror that I'd been found."What's the password?" a familiar boy's voice bellowed out. My shoulders relaxed and I exhaled with relief, but I stayed inside the tree.

"Nirvana," I replied, happy to hear a friendly voice as he crawled into the den and sat beside me.

"What are you doing here on your own, L.J., and where are your shoes?" I moved toward the daylight slowly and let him see part of my face.

"How bad is it? Do I look like Freddy Kruger?" I waited for his response, my eyebrows pulling together, and my lip quivering. He stared at me with his mouth wide open, then reached for the cigarettes and couldn't find them. I reached inside my pocket and handed them to him along with the matches.

"L.J., you don't smoke." He looked at me in surprise.

"I do now." I reached for the packet and took another out. "What do you need me to do?" He cleared his throat while taking off his shoes, then showed me his fluffy brown socks, which he was about to give me. He was tall and thin with brown hair and brown eyes; his eyelashes were so long. I'd looked into those eyes since I was three years old. We'd always been together. At nursery, we pretended to get married. Aged four, he'd shown me his penis because he said it felt funny, and I'd bandaged it up using the first aid kit.

"Thank you. I hope your feet don't stink." I raised a half smile and snorted a laugh.

"They will do when you've worn them," he jested, and punched my arm gently, winking at me with humour.

He then pulled a bottle of alcohol out of his wax jacket and handed it to me."What is it?" I looked at him, shocked.

"Drink some. You'll feel better, and it'll warm you up." He pushed it into my free hand, and I took the top off to smell it, while trying to hold a cigarette at the same time—very uncoordinated.

"It smells like old farts!" I looked at him and started to laugh. I trusted him, so took a swig; it burnt the back of my throat and I spat most of it out all over us. He took the bottle from me and rolled his eyes.

"Watch and learn." He swigged the bottle and gulped loudly."It'll stop the pain," he said, handing it back to me. I tried again, and this time let the burning liquid roll over my tongue and down my throat. Feeling it warming my stomach was surprisingly comforting."It's whisky; I nicked it from my dad's bar!" He beamed at me, knowing that it'd taken the edge off the pain I was feeling.

"It really is horrible stuff." I stuck my tongue out like it'd been stung by a bee and wrinkled my nose.

"L.J., it's your dad again, isn't it?" He frowned, and I nodded. He reached out to cuddle me and I embraced it—he made me feel safe. "I'll stay with you for as long as I can," he said reassuringly, handing me the whisky.

"I hate him," I said, exhaling the cigarette smoke into the air. He squeezed my hand and took another swig.

"I hate my parents too. Don't worry. We'll be adults soon, and we can get the f*ck out of there." He put his arm around me again and pulled me closer to get warm. I looked at my feet and pulled one of his socks off my foot for him to wear.

"Sock buddies for life!" I handed it to him, nipping my nose. "Are we drunk?" I asked, hiccupping, and starting to giggle, feeling more relaxed now.

"Save some for me!" A voice came out of nowhere, making us jump, then another familiar voice, one after another; it was the gang. "Jesus, L.J., what happened to your face?" I dropped my head then looked to my friend, and he explained what'd happened.

"The police are at your house; we wondered what was going on," one of my girlfriends said, taking her jumper off to put on me as I was clearly shaking again, now from fear. Stacy was so beautiful with her thick black curls and big baby blue eyes. She was always so calm and cool; I really looked up to her, and she made me laugh so much. "We'll all look after you." She smiled, pulling food out of my hair and taking off her shoe, then sock, and placing it on my bare foot, which was now turning purple with the cold.

Faces stared at me as I came out of the tree stump; they surrounded me but didn't know what to say. We sat together on the floor trying to work out what to do.

"My dad gets rid of rats by putting poison in the cheese; try that. How will anyone ever know?" was one suggestion.

"Who's got some fake ID to get more booze?" I shouted, then rested my head on Stacy's shoulder."I want to get drunk! I kind of like alcohol." I grinned and hiccupped again.

"You can stay at mine; I'll hide you in my attic. I can get more booze and cigs, and we can watch Dirty Dancing." She kissed my head and squeezed my hand, and with my eyes I said thank you.

"What are you going to do if you have to go back there, L.J.?" one of the members of the group asked.

"I don't know," I responded honestly, my lip quivering."Hopefully he'll have choked on his f*cking precious meat and potato pie!"

CHAPTER TWO

"I got one less problem without ya." ~ Ariana Grande

After the 'pie in the face' fiasco, I was made to go back to the house. The police were lied to, and I was classed as a teenage 'runaway'. Because they weren't told the truth, social services didn't get involved. It was too much of a family embarrassment for my mother, so she just brushed it under the carpet and kept an extra-watchful eye over me. I had no respect for her from that day on and was filled with anger toward them both.

I was determined to get out of that house as fast as I could. If that wasn't enough of a warning sign for my mother to leave her marriage, nothing would be. I began a cunning action plan in the hope that he would go. I was going to be the worst stepdaughter imaginable, to cause as much friction between them as possible, coupled with immense clinginess to my mother so that I would take all her affection away from him.

I put booby traps everywhere for him, hoping he would fall and break his fat face. I left drawing pins under his cushion for when he sat his lazy ass down and put laxatives in his tea on a regular basis, so he'd be locked in the toilet, and we didn't have to talk to him. I hated him with a passion. My friends did, too. Whenever I went to meet them with a black eye, they slashed his van tyres and stuck socks up his exhaust pipe. I knew they had my back.

The plan was smart, bullet-proof: I would do well at school, get my A-levels, and move out to go to university to study for a degree in journalism, travel the world writing about anything and everything, meet the man of my dreams, move into a castle, win an Oscar for my creative flair, and have enough money to divorce my entire family!

Unfortunately, it didn't quite go according to plan. My stepdad did move out, but only after cheating on my mum and taking her for every last penny. I've not seen him again to this day; he went into hiding for his crimes, I guess.

I worked hard at school, got my A levels, and went to university, but wasn't smart enough to do journalism, so I settled for psychology. I got my degree, met a guy, and bought a house. I got a good job, got bored of the guy, met my husband, and bought a different house. We had a baby girl, I adopted his stepson, then we had another child—a baby boy. He sat in one corner of the house, and I sat in another. We had nothing in common, and I was permanently annoyed by him and bored. Then I found him cheating.

"What the f*ck are you doing with your wedding dress, L.J.?" my husband yelled at me, putting both his hands on his head.

"What does it look like I'm doing? You cheating f*cking asshole! How could you? I've given up my life for you, to raise our kids. Do you know how embarrassing it is being married to the local drunk? Now this. I'll be a laughingstock! And our kids? How have you had an affair when you can't even get it up because you're so pissed all the time? She is the reason we haven't had sex for a year, isn't she? Too busy poking another hole?" My hands gripped the wedding dress so tightly they formed a fist.

"She meant nothing. It was just a mistake. Look, don't do it. L.J., you'll regret it. You love that dress." He looked worried as I held my beautiful princess fairy tale wedding dress close to the open fire in our living room. I knew I was going to do it; it was symbolic to me—a bold statement.

"Meant nothing? A mistake? Oh, I'm sorry, did you accidently fall over, and your dick just somehow magically fell into her fat f*cking vagina?" I trembled with rage and screamed my words out, but the neighbours were used to our fights; we'd been having them for months now.
"I never slept with her. We just talked." He tried badly to convince me. I could see the guilt written all over his face.

"An emotional affair?" I snorted."Yeah, whatever, I've read the emails. You can't worm your sneaky little way out of this one," I hissed with venom on my tongue.

"What's an emotional affair?" He scratched his head, and I rolled my eyes.

"Stop pretending to be stupid. You talked for six months. Here, let me refresh your memory… 'I can't wait to see you and be with you again in my arms.' Would you like me to quote anymore from the trails of emails between you? Oh, here's a classic: 'I love you and miss you so much. We'll be together soon!' Stop f*cking lying to me, I know everything!"

"I don't love her; it's just words," he said, hanging his head in shame.

"So were our marriage vows, apparently," I said with disappointment, and let go of my wedding dress, dropping it onto the fire. It ignited instantly and was engulfed in raging flames.

"Jesus, you'll burn the house down, you crazy bitch!" he screamed at me."Help me put this out. Are you trying to get us both killed? I'll have you done for arson!" He panicked and stamped out what had been consumed by fire.

"Oh, you really do care, don't you? Have me arrested? Such kind words of love," I said, amused, watching him now looking completely terrified.

"This is not you. L.J., you're timid, you never fight back. This attitude doesn't suit you," he said, out of breath, coughing, and opening windows, rushing to the kitchen to get some water to put out the burning dress.

"Well, if a person gets pushed hard enough, they do unexpected things." I felt a sudden urge to help him, but then thought better of it.

"You can't be on your own. You never have been, and you won't cope," he continued."You have no money, no place to go, and I'm not letting you take my kids away from me." He started to get angry.

"You just watch me! I was always too good for you, and I will do just fine," I snapped, my head racing. I had no plan.

"Who's going to help you? Your family? Like they give a sh*t. They always let you down. All you have is me." He knew exactly how to hit me to make me feel less powerful."They're all crazy like you. I don't want them near my kids."

"Your own mother and father warned me not to marry you. They said their own son was an alcoholic who would never change, so touché!" I let out a slightly manic laugh at the realisation that they were right.

I moved toward him and looked him right in his eyes."F*ck you and f*ck our marriage! I hope the house burns down with you in it!" I pushed him out of my path and grabbed my suitcase, already packed with the kids' things.

"I'm getting the kids from your mum's and I'm not coming back." I gritted my teeth in anger at him and got my phone out of my pocket. Scrolling through photos, I found one of the woman he'd been cheating with, which I'd saved when I'd stalked her on social media. I held the phone up to him with her image on the screen. She was a larger girl with jet black hair, her tits hanging out, and tattoos everywhere. Not attractive, rough around the edges, and terrible teeth; she looked like someone out of Shameless.

"Pretty girl, isn't she?" I said with sarcasm."Take one good hard look at me, and never forget what you've lost. I'm relieved I don't have to be associated with you anymore, and the chances are I might actually get a good f*ck now! I should've left you years ago." I tossed my hair back, slipped into my shoes, and walked toward the door, reaching for my car keys.

I looked at my wedding dress, now a pile of half-burnt, half-soggy material on the fire. What was once a brilliant white, beautiful dress was now black and scolded, like my heart. The room smelt of its fumes, and I felt sad. He fell to the floor on his knees and started to cry."Stop crying, you'll give yourself a nosebleed." I gulped, trying not to fall for his emotional manipulation.

"Stay. We can work through this, L.J. You're my wife," he begged.

"Don't you DARE call me your wife," I snapped, leaning against the wall, my heart beating and my ears ringing from the stress."For better or for worse? I've changed your f*cking underwear when you've been that drunk you've pissed and sh*t yourself. I stood by you. For richer or for poorer? I had everything before I met you. Your addiction made us poor; you took food out of our children's mouths and bought alcohol. I starved because of you, yet I still stood by you."

"To love and to cherish, till death do us part, according to God's holy law.' Vows—they mean nothing to you. I fulfilled mine. Now I want a divorce. This was ten years too long."

I looked at my left hand and my wedding ring and engagement ring and slowly took them both off."Here, have them back. They mean nothing now. Sell them and buy yourself some more f*cking beer; that's who you're really married to!"

I took one last look at him to confirm I was understood, opened the door, and I was gone.

CHAPTER THREE

"Freedom" ~ George Michael

No one can explain how fantastic and alive you feel when you shed someone you've lived with who has been sapping all your positive energy. When you're tied to the wrong person it weighs you down more than you realise; your identity fades, and you have no voice. It felt like I was tied to a rock at the bottom of the ocean for years. Now, I was swimming free and doing backflips, letting the wonderful ocean of life wash over me.

I felt and looked amazing, every part of me charged with an invisible force field of energy. I got up every day and couldn't wait to see what it was going to deliver. I was so happy. My little house was filled with my stuff, and I could do whatever I wanted in it—be messy, loud, and as silly as I liked. I didn't have to run around after anyone cleaning up their mess, and I had my own remote to watch TV, if I wanted to, which wasn't very often as I was never in. I even bought myself a little Jack Russell puppy to join our crazy little family. My ex-husband hated animals, so I was never allowed one. 'Allowed one,' can you believe that? Another adult saying,"No, you can't." I'd been so controlled for years.

After a few months of being alone and settling into a new routine, I'd hit the online dating scene and was never on my own on the weekends when I didn't have the kids. My body was in the best shape it'd ever been. I'm talking six-pack, toned legs, and perfectly pert tits. I felt incredible. I got my hair and tan done on a regular basis, so always looked like a goddess in case I had a date. I'd got my confidence back. I was me again. I'd really missed myself.

How could anyone want to be married when you have so much choice? I loved living by myself; my attitude had completely changed. I had a part-time job, got some child support from the ex, and seemed to just about cope with money. I was a terrible cook, but there was always takeout, and I'd pretty much looked after everyone by myself for the past ten years anyway; he never did anything in the house to help. I'd basically been another mother to him. He went out to work and left me with two jobs, effectively. No wonder I'd always been so tired. Now, if something didn't get done, I wasn't made to feel bad or wear myself out trying to please anyone.

I know that eating healthily, looking after your body, and getting regular fresh air is great for the mind, body, and soul, but I'd discovered something even better—SEX! I'm not talking a quicky, 'wham bam, thank you ma'am,' I'm talking naughty, filthy, spontaneous, HOT sex. I had my very own f*ck buddy! He was a bit of an enigma. I really didn't understand him, but he'd been teaching me how to f*ck. I knew all the fundamental things, I knew what to do to have sex, but really enjoying sex was an entirely different thing.

I was living like a queen. I had my own place, my own money, and I had this guy who didn't want any attachment to me, who blew my mind and my vagina on a regular basis. It was almost like an exciting game; he pulled me in, then pushed me away, then knew he needed the sex just as bad as me, so he hooked me back in. I'd play hard to get, acting all vulnerable and innocent, pretending to have absolutely no idea what he was doing, so I could be seduced and dominated by him. We were both as bad as each other, playing a game of cat and mouse.

I nicknamed him 'Fancy Pants' as he was posh and fancy. He was also good looking and knew it. He had a big, detached house with nice things, and a black cat that used to unnerve me as it used to spy on us having sex.

When we weren't f*cking in his house, we were sexting all night long, winding each other up, and sending videos and photos of ourselves doing perverted things. Most importantly, he made me laugh harder than anyone had ever done in my life, and he seemed to bring out this little devil in me. He unearthed a nymphomaniac. I got such a high from f*cking him, I'm surprised I didn't fly through his roof!

I started to write a journal of all the thoughts I was having about him, because they flooded me. I couldn't get enough of the things he was teaching me; it was like I'd been sexually brainwashed, and I was stuck in a world of sexstasy.

I became funny too, or I'd always been funny, and he just brought that out in me. Together we were an explosion of exhilarating, blushful, childlike, free spirits.

I'd never had sex like this with anyone; in fact, I don't think I'd ever had a proper orgasm until I had sex with Fancy Pants. How I was married for ten years and missed out on this I don't know, but I'd definitely not been having good sex in my marriage or with any of my previous partners. I know that they say you can get addicted to drugs and alcohol, but I was now addicted to sex—with him.

This arrangement went on for about a year before he started to withdraw. I heard less and less of him and started to realise how much I missed our interactions. I'd text, he'd read the message, and ignore me. So, I'd text again and again until I got a reply. Then he blocked me. I'd be on the dating sites, and he was there chatting up other women, and I was so confused. I hadn't trapped him or said anything bad to him, yet he was acting so odd.

"Oi! Wabbit, why are you hiding from me?" I sent a voice recording through 'Plenty of Fish' and waited an age to get a response.

"You've got too much for me," he replied coldly, and I was shocked.

"What do you mean? We've not seen each other for ages," I replied, dumbfounded.

"L.J., you're too clingy, needy, and you text all the time. Don't you have a job?" He was now being rude.

"No, I'm not, I just like the fun we have." I felt insecure and puzzled.

"We had an agreement—just sex, nothing more. I'm not looking for a relationship." He put lots of exclamation marks after his text.

"Neither am I; I've just come out of a marriage. I'm sorry, I guess I'm just new to the rules and regulations of a f*ck buddy. Bye, then. Have fun." I signed off and threw my phone onto the bed. It pinged almost immediately with another message from him. I expected a 'goodbye, it was nice knowing you.'

"Look, if you can promise that's all it is then get over here now (oi… and bring your wabbit)!"

"I'll be ten minutes!" I leapt off the bed, threw on my jeans and t-shirt, grabbed my heels and bag, and ran across the house to get to the car. Driving with one hand on the wheel, the other in my make-up bag, I made myself look presentable, my heart thumping out of my chest. When I got to the door, he was smiling from ear to ear and giggling to himself."What are you laughing at?" I smiled widely back.

"Your top's on the wrong way round and inside out; in a rush, were you?" He shook his head and continued to smile at me, showing his sexy, perfectly white teeth.

"It's just sex," I reaffirmed, and kicked off my heels.

"Is it now?" He looked at me with cautious eyes.

"Swear it is, cross my heart." I did the crucifix sign and kissed two of my fingers.

He moved into me and looked at my top, smirking."Take it off," he instructed.

"You take it off," I replied playfully. He then ripped open the top with his bare hands and looked at my breasts.

"What am I going to drive home in now?" I snorted, looking at the tattered t-shirt.

"I'll lend you one of my old rags, Cinderella." He pushed me against the staircase and started to kiss my neck and breasts.

"I'll leave you a shoe, Prince Fancy Pants," I giggled."So," I said, walking backward away from him toward the stairs."What are you going to do with me tonight?" I bit my lip and squeezed his penis gently through his tight jeans.

"Where's your wabbit?" he said emotionlessly, but his eyes burnt through me. I directed him with my eyes to my bag on the floor."Turn around," he said gently, and I did."I'm going to f*ck you here." He smacked my bottom hard."While your wabbit is inside here." He put his hands down my pants and stuck his finger inside me.

"But what if my wabbit suffocates? I'm not sure about animal rights here?" I giggled and waited for him to laugh, but he rolled his eyes at me.

"Shut up and get up those stairs." He walked toward me, backing me onto the stairs.

"Your room again? Can't we do it outside in the garden? It's nice weather…" Before I could say another word, he was kissing me, and telling me again to shut up."We never talk," I said, putting my hands in the air and giggling into his mouth. Our eyes locked and we were both desperate for one another.

"I love this," he said, looking up at me, starry-eyed.

"I love it too. Now, come on, you're wasting valuable shagging time, you big STUD!" And he ran up the stairs after me.

We got to his room, he pushed me onto the bed, pulled off my jeans, and went down on me with one hand over my mouth."I can't breathe," I said, muffled, through his hand, and he removed it, knowing he'd made his point.

Getting up to shut the bedroom door, he took off his belt and said,"Now turn around and bend over, Mr Wabbit needs to go back in his hole." I felt them both slide inside me at the same time and gave out a scream. He kissed me all over my body as he slowly took advantage of me and made me watch through the mirrors in his room.

"Oh L.J., what am I going to do with you?" He flipped me over and kissed me hard. I didn't answer him, but my head told me that I wanted him to fall in love with me. I knew from that moment on that it was more to me than it was to him, but if I had to lie to keep this wonderful situationship going, then I'd tell the biggest, fattest lies ever.

Hopefully, one day, he'd wake up and have feelings, not just a hardon for me, I thought, while he pulled me down the bed to the edge to f*ck again.

I turned to the side and saw a plate with some kind of half-eaten cake."You could've at least tidied up before I got here," I mocked him. He looked at the plate and grabbed it, putting it down on the floor. Little did I know that he had the cake in his hand. He smeared it all over my breasts and started to lick it off.

"Sorry, I'll just clear my plate." He laughed into my breasts and looked up at me for a reaction, then kissed me.

"Mmmm, that's yummy, what is it?" I quizzed, wiping bits of cake off my face.

"Tiramisu. It means to pick me up, or cheer you up," he said in a thick Italian accent.

"Well, it's certainly sticky." We both laughed and kissed. The strong coffee and cream rolled over our entwined tongues, and before I knew it, we were making love, and I'd gone right back to the stars on a rocket ship.

CHAPTER FOUR

"Unstoppable" ~ Sia

I got off the busy train at Manchester Victoria and pushed my way through the crowd of commuters to get to the office. I'd worked for this company after graduating, and when the managing director found out I was available again, he re-hired me part-time. It'd been ten years since I'd been in an office; my days had comprised changing nappies and doing school runs, baking, painting, reading, and teaching the children. I'd been trapped in the home, but I would never regret the love and attention I put into them. Also, their dad was completely unreliable, and I was terrified of him picking them up from nursery drunk and the house burning down, so I'd had no choice but to protect them.

Twelve months on and what was once a busy office had been reduced to just three people. The business was doing badly, and I'd been set the task to try to bring it back to life. It was a struggle, but we were slowly getting there. I walked into the office, hung up my coat, and headed toward the coffee machine."Morning, L.J.," a voice came from behind me; it was one of the managers from the London office.

"Gosh, you made me jump. Good morning! What are you doing here?" I reached for a paper towel to clean up the spilt coffee.

"We're all in the meeting room, when you're ready." He tapped his foot and looked at his watch impatiently.

"Okay, coming right now." I followed him, grabbing a pen and paper. He never turned up unless it was to discuss financial things or to sack someone. I joined the other two members of staff who sat there looking worried and pale.

"It's with our deepest regret we inform you that we intend to shut down the Manchester office," he said, calculated, with no remorse.

"WHAT THE F*CK?" I shouted, spitting my coffee out."Manchester's been open nearly 30 years. You can't shut it down. What about our reputation in the marketplace?" I said with fighting spirit.

"Calm down, L.J. We're giving you a redundancy package." He shuffled some papers around and cleared his throat. I stood up and paced around the room.

"What are our other options? A transfer to another branch?" I put my hands through my hair, trying to work out how I'd manage childcare from another branch.

"I'm afraid we have no other options for you." The room went deadly silent.

"So, what you're really saying is you're firing the lot of us?" I put my hands on my hips and stared right into his eyes, looking for the real answer.

"You're being made redundant with immediate effect. Each of you has an envelope with your expected pay for the end of the month." He handed them across the table.

"F*ck this, it's bullsh*t. I won't be needing a reference," I said, taking my letter and opening it to see what I was going to be paid."Seriously,

I might as well wipe my ass with this." I tore the letter up and threw it in his face, then turned to the other two employees who were open-mouthed and in shock."Been nice working with you."

I went to my desk and gathered my personal belongings: photos of the kids, loose change, a red lipstick, and some heels. I got a mirror out of my bag, then checked my phone to find a missed call and a few text messages. One was from the managing director with a message saying,"Call me," which I ignored, and one was from Fancy Pants saying,"It's over, for good." I looked in the mirror, applied my red lipstick, pursed my lips together, slipped into my heels, and put on my long, black, smart coat.

I walked to the elevator and got in. Looking at my reflection in the mirror, I saw myself from every angle—my red lips, my long hair. I stared at myself while the elevator went down, then I let out a loud scream of frustration."Well, this was not part of the plan," I said to my reflection, my mind racing, thinking of ways to feed my children and pay my bills."What the f*ck am I going to do now?" My lip started to quiver, and I was about to burst into tears when my phone pinged again; it was Fancy Pants. I pressed dial and called him. It went straight to voicemail, as it always did.

"I got your message. I was just made redundant at the same time you decided to tell me it was over, again. Look, I really liked you, but it's your choice. I can't force you to stay with me. I'll miss you. It was fun." I took a deep breath, then said goodbye and hung up. I don't know how I got to the train station, but standing on the platform I suddenly felt vulnerable and unsure about the future. I looked all around me. Advertising banners were everywhere, and billboards filled with images of beautiful, successful people, living a better life than me: a broke single mum with no job, no prospects, no boyfriend, and no one to f*ck.

All the latest movies and books being released were featured, as were fitness adverts, holidays, and beauty products. I looked at the billboard behind me and my mind started to race—the bestselling book, Fifty Shades of Grey, was plastered all over it. I've read these books, I thought, and my sex life's been way hotter than that; maybe I should write about mine? The journal I've been writing, I already have lots of notes; I could use them. I creased my face up to the irony that my amazing sex life was now over.

I could put a naughty book together. How hard could it be to get published? I stared at the book advert until my train arrived, and I got on. I'd have six weeks to find a job before my redundancy pay ran out; could a book be written in that time?"This is an amazing idea," I repeated to myself, filling my heart and my head with hope. E.L. James is a multi-millionaire, and it's made up; what would people pay for the real thing?"This is a fantastic business idea—add in humour, a bit about a dog, and I'm the next William f*cking Shakespeare," I said under my breath.

I got my phone out of my bag and started to text Fancy Pants."I know what I'm going to do. I know how I'm going to turn my life around." I texted with love hearts and smiley face emojis and sent it, hoping he'd reply.

"Go on, but make it quick, some of us have to work." He was so rude. I scrunched my face up and stuck my tongue out at the phone.

"Remember the Fifty Shades movies?"

"Yes, they were tame. Why?"

"What if I wrote about our sexual experiences, not mentioning your name, and showed the world how to really f*ck? It's genius! If she got rich making up a steamy sex story, imagine how people would react to the real thing? Our experience has been incredible; why not share it with the world? It's guaranteed money, right?"

"L.J., it's ridiculous. You're not going to be able to write a book. You're in the clouds; perhaps a little bit of shock from today? If you write a book, I'll suck my own cock!"

"But that's impossible," I replied confused, rolling my eyes.

"Exactly. Now look, I need you to stop texting me. Okay?" Within seconds I was blocked. For a fleeting moment I thought he was right, and doubt set in my mind, then a switch inside me flicked. I will show you that I can write a book. You can stick your fancy house, your fancy car, and your fancy, boring job, right up your asshole, I thought, angry at his dismissal and complete disregard for my feelings. He made me feel rejected, unimportant, and cheap.

I looked out of the train window at everything passing by. I felt deep inside like a bell had been rung. It was an awakening within me; something almost spiritual was bubbling inside. I was going to tell my story, the whole truth, and nothing but the truth. I practically ran through my front door and was greeted by an insane dog following me and licking me to death."Hello, sweetheart, at least you're always pleased to see me!" I kissed him and squeezed him with affection. I fed him and walked to my room to get my journal. Flicking through the past years, all my dates, where I'd been, and whom I'd met along the way, none were as exciting and sexual as Mr Fancy Pants.

I read through the notes. I'd nicknamed all the men something after I'd been on dates, and it was quite amusing to read back. Mr Strawberry Psychopath, The Leprechaun, Mr Star Wars, to name a few. The online dating scene, its ups and downs, dick pics, dangers, fake people, and my dreams and sexual fantasies had all been logged in a one-year journal."A Year of Online Dating," I said out loud, then flicked through more pages, and one stood out. I'd written in red lipstick across the entire page,"I LOVE TIRAMISU." I closed my eyes and remembered Fancy Pants eating it off me. Getting a plain sheet of paper, I wrote,"A Year of Tiramisu" at the top of the page and smiled to myself; it was unusual, but powerful, and I just knew it was right.

The dog jumped onto my bed and crumpled my journal."A Year of Tiramisu. What do you think, Gibson?" My dog barked and licked my face, jumping all over me."I take it that's your seal of approval?" Grabbing his little paw, we shook on it, and I laid back on my bed and looked at my bedroom ceiling. My head was full of ideas."Well, Fancy Pants, I guess you're going to be sucking your own cock!"

CHAPTER FIVE

"Starving" ~ Hailee Steinfeld

The next six weeks of my life I will remember on my death bed, and thank the lord for my amazing experience. Nothing could take it away from me, change it, or make it feel any different. I completely lost the plot in the most amazingly creative way. Writing turned me on way more than any man ever could—I was on fire. Every part of me was in tune with myself. I noticed everything around me more; things even smelt and tasted differently. I became fully aware of myself, charged and alive for the first time. I'd found my true love, and it was to write.

Now, typically, all writers have a plan. They have structure, know what they're going to do before they write, are well read on the subject, know what their competition is, and what they can and cannot put into the content without legal implications. I was fearless, I was Indiana f*cking Jones diving in at the deep end, not scared of anything. What I was writing was the truth, and if people didn't like it, they didn't have to read it. I had no filter. I didn't care.

I sat at my kitchen table for the best part of twelve hours a day for six weeks. I had to break off for children and the everyday drudge, and on the weekends when I didn't have the kids I barely slept, was constantly drinking wine to inspire me, and I worked solidly. I closed my eyes and went back in time to the first night I logged onto dating apps and exchanged messages with strangers. I remembered the buzz of the attention I got from all walks of life telling me how pretty I was and that they would love a date. My mind visualised and recalled the conversations I'd had, and my fingers couldn't type fast enough on the keyboard. It was both overwhelming and addictive.

What made it so easy was that these were real conversations, characters on the page who I'd met or made love to in my new world of singledom, which was exciting enough without the fact that for twelve full months I had an absolute ball of a time—wild, footloose, and panty-free.

I offered a bit of background and introduced Fancy Pants to my potential readers—that's when my story got interesting. This man had got me hooked, so I had to get the reader hooked on him too—make them feel the attraction. But they also had to see that he was a bit of a bad boy. If he was going to read it, I couldn't hurt his feelings too much, so I would make out to the world that he was a sex god in the bedroom, which was the truth, but in all honesty, until him I'd had very little sexual experience to compare it to.

Most of the time, before actually writing the chapter, all I had to do was close my eyes and recall a moment or particular sexual encounter I'd had with him, sometimes even masturbate, and it was like I was back in the room with him; I could see him in front of me, I could look into his eyes, and I could feel his touch, smell him, and taste him. It was some strange kind of virtual reality that I could tap into at any point I wanted—like I had a time machine.

I remembered his words and how he said them, and I'd kept all his hilarious, cheeky texts. I used these to help me compose the story, but most of the recall was on an emotionally heightened level I'd never experienced before. I suppose one could compare it to being spiritually high, having an out of body experience, or a dissociative episode. Whatever it was, it was working, and the book was charged with exciting, exhilarating moments from my sex life.

I spent my days laughing at the words coming into my mind, the sexual hiccups, and shocks I'd encountered with this man, the highs, and the lows. But then I could also see that the book was forming an undercurrent—it was turning into a love story, a rather silly love story, but a love story, nonetheless. This story was not only coming from my creative mind and experience, but it was also coming from my heart. I was falling for him, unhealthily, perhaps obsessively even.

I'd written everything up until our last meeting, then ran out of things to say. I didn't know how to end it. I needed more time with him. I looked up at the time and I'd not moved from my seat for hours."Time to take a break. Come with me to the shop to get some wine?" I tickled the dog's chin and he got excited, knowing we were going out for a walk. 'Ping', my phone alerted me; it was a Facebook notification from Fancy Pants. I froze to the spot. I'd really believed him when he'd said he didn't want to speak to me again. It read:"Fancy a F*ck?"

I shrugged and shook my head. He's got some balls after how he treated me. Then I thought, maybe it's time you got a taste of your own medicine, Mr Fancy wanker Pants. Maybe I will use you for sex to finish the book! Reluctantly, I decided to reply,"Say 8.30pm?" No kisses, totally unemotional. I knew I was a booty call.

"Looking forward to it, don't be late," he replied with a kiss. He was clearly drunk.

"Oh my god, I'm officially just as bad as him," I uttered to myself in disbelief. I dashed to the corner shop in the rain with the dog and grabbed a bottle of wine. I was going to need a drink before committing this disingenuous act. Instead of having longing lustful loving thoughts about him, I was going to be taking mental notes for research. Even though I knew he was using me, two wrongs don't make a right, and I felt guilty and selfish. I vowed to myself that this would be the book ending, the final chapter, and I wouldn't do this again. I didn't know I was capable of this; perhaps I was going mad?

I booked a cab, jumped into the shower, and washed quickly, thinking of what to wear. I had to wear something mind-blowing for our last time together; perhaps a little red dress and some stilettoes? I love red; my lips were always covered in red. By the time I was ready I'd drunk a full bottle of wine and realised I was drunk having not eaten anything all day. This would be interesting! Cab. Doorbell. Greeting. Fancy Pants.

"L.J." He smiled and let me walk through his front door."You look nice! Had your hair done?" he complimented me.

"It's just a bit darker," I said, looking straight past him."New kitchen?" I continued, keeping my heart from pounding out of my chest.

"Just a few alterations," he replied calmly.

"Hiccup," came out of my mouth, and I swayed.

"Have you been drinking?"

"No. Hiccup, hiccup. Well, maybe slightly," I stopped lying and pulled my dress up and over my head, throwing it to the floor, showing my red lace underwear."Well, are you going to f*ck me or not?" I put my hands in the air in confusion.

"Coffee first, and perhaps something to eat?" He picked up my dress and handed it to me, chuckling to himself while he filled the kettle."Come on then, shout at me. I know you're mad." He exhaled as if he was getting ready for some bad news.

"I'm not—hiccup—mad. I'm disappointed," I said after a long pause.

He handed me a coffee and pushed the sugar bowl and spoon toward me."Go on." He stared at the floor.

"You're up and down, hot and cold, wonderful then a bastard; you're giving we whiplash with your moods. We were having so much fun then you just cut me out and it's been seven weeks since I've heard a word from you, only to receive a text saying, 'Fancy a f*ck?' Do you think I'm some kind of prostitute? An easy lay? You don't seem to have any respect for me or even believe in me?" I rushed all the words out dramatically."You make me so happy, but also so bloody mad!"

"I don't think you're a prostitute, and I do really like you." He moved toward me and kissed me on the head.

"Like me or love me?" I looked into his eyes and saw he didn't have an answer."Why are you avoiding the question?" I pushed him away.

"Hiccups gone now?" His smile told me I'd just had Polish coffee.

"It tasted awful." I blurted out a nervous laugh and wiped away my angry tears."I've written most of that book I was telling you about. I should have it finished in a few more weeks," I bragged."It's about us and what we've got up to in the bedroom—total filth!"

"Well done! I could have the next J.K. Rowling stood in my kitchen. I'm pleased for you. I have to say there isn't much left for us to do. We've done everything." He put his hands around my waist and looked at my half-naked body with desire.

"Well, I don't know. We haven't done the butterfly."

"Yes, we have; remember, front room on the side table?" I looked at him, amazed at his instant recall."Countertop, happy scissors, seated scissors, hands behind ankles, the kinky missionary, the yab-yum with a twist on the sofa?" I looked at him wide eyes in amazement.

"You read Cosmopolitan? Do you paint your nails too?" I grabbed his hand and looked for evidence, giggling."We haven't done the reverse slither." He grabbed his phone and googled it.

"I don't think you get maximum benefit from that one." He rubbed his chin."Look, we've not done this; it's called the circus freak." He showed me a photo of a woman standing up, one leg on the floor and one leg up, her foot resting on his shoulder.

"Fancy Pants, I'll fall over. I'm not a Barbie doll! No way I'm flexible enough." I pushed the phone away."Anyway, you'll have to catch me first." I ran to the other side of the kitchen table and wiggled my bum while waiting for his next move. He chased me; I screamed and ran into the front room playfully.

"When I catch you, I'm going to spank your ass, L.J."

"I surrender!" I laughed loudly and rushed over to kiss him."Don't leave me again," I said, pulling his hair through my fingers.

"Shut up and get upstairs." He smacked my bottom hard, and I yelped. We walked up the stairs and closed the door. After that night, I never wanted to leave him again.

CHAPTER SIX

"Help!" ~ The Beatles

"Start, you piece of sh*t car—start!" I kicked it with my foot then hopped up and down with pain. I'd found a new job, but it was miles away, and they'd taken a risk on me because I told them they couldn't have a reference from my last employer. It was low paid and not my thing, but I was desperate. Working in the engineering recruitment industry was new, and I had no idea what I was doing. Every day I faked it to make it, and I was completely useless.

"I'm sorry I'm late, I couldn't get the car to start," I bellowed into the office as I entered the room. There were no women employed at the office apart from me, and I used it to my advantage by always wearing the tightest clothes, which accentuated my body. Most days it worked, but today it didn't.

"Well, you can work through your lunch." My boss looked over to me and scowled coldly.

"Jesus, I'm ten minutes late." I snorted and laughed.

"In the meeting room, NOW." He stood and waited for me to acknowledge him. I looked at him with my 'don't f*ck with me' eyes.

"Erm, sorry to interrupt, but Fox is on the line asking for L.J.," a nervous intern delicately whispered across the room to the manager.

"It's a client and a candidate, the world of business doesn't stop because my car broke down, right? I should take the call." I put my hand on my hips, and everyone put their heads down to work as the manager's face got redder and redder with rage."Just put it through, sweetie." I blew a bubble with my bubble gum, stared the manager out, and waited for him to transfer the call, standing tall and holding my own. He was my age; I wouldn't be talked to like a child. The manager nodded to the intern and the call was transferred.

"Hi, you're through to L.J., is this Fox?" I spoke confidently.

"It is indeed. How are you today?" a thick Liverpudlian accent replied, and my first impression was that he had a manly, sexy voice. We'd been back and forth with exchanges for nearly three months; he was high up in the industry and impossible to reach.

"Thank you for completing the registration form I sent through to you. I just have a few more questions."

"Fire away!"

"What's your expected yearly salary, and what do you need to match on bonus, company car, and commission?" My inner dialogue asked, are you single and would you like to come and take me over this desk.

"Ninety thousand, BMW, bonus and commission needs to be exceptional, but I'm looking for the right role more than anything," he said confidently. I was bringing in 20k a year and half of that went on childcare. How the other half live, I thought.

"Any other expectations that I've missed?" I questioned further.

"How about dinner?" he flirted, and I blushed down the phone.

"I'd love to." I beamed down the phone without a second thought. His voice felt so familiar to me."But let's keep it our little secret," I whispered.

"I like to know who I'm dealing with. It's always better to meet face-to-face I feel," he said, perhaps as an afterthought.

"How about a client visit? On the form you said you also need staff at your current company. I'll be very discreet!" I looked at the screen, reading the notes he'd made.

"We don't usually work with recruiters—we have a large response locally, but I'll make this one exception." He was so charming.

"Fantastic. What date and time is best for you?" I looked at my calendar to see where I could fit him in, and it was empty. I jumped at the chance to get out of the office and on the road, away from my sh*t of a boss.

"Tomorrow too soon? 4.30pm, Birmingham office?" I looked at my boss and tried to get his attention, waving across the room.

"Fox, can I just put you on hold for a second please so I can confirm with management that I can attend?"

"No problem." He waited on hold.

"Boss, can I attend a client visit in Birmingham tomorrow at 4.30? It's informal I think, so I'll be fine by myself." I shook the phone in the air."He's on hold, needs an answer now," I pushed for an answer eagerly.

"Make sure you bring back business," he snapped, and I thought, what an asshole, as I went back to Fox to confirm."Fox, are you still there?" I smiled down the phone.

"I am." His sexy voice seemed even more attractive as time went on talking to him.

"I can attend, and I will bring you a list of jobs we have that might be suitable for you. Do I need to prepare anything for the meeting?" I typed my notes onto the computer, holding the phone to my ear with my shoulder.

"A full presentation of your knowledge of my company, and what you can do for us, with some supporting CVs, on PowerPoint please," he demanded, and I stared at my screen in shock.

"You're kidding, right?" I snorted a nervous laugh down the phone.

"I never joke about business," he said coldly.

"Right, okay. It's done." My heart pounded with stress. I'd done no research on his company, but I did have some jobs that he might be interested in, and a few CVs from people who would be suitable to work for him. I was in for a long night of work. The phones were ringing off the hook and consultants all around me were talking loudly, making their sales pitches.

"Fox, I'm just going to transfer the call to our boardroom, I'm having trouble hearing you," I bellowed out into the office, putting my finger in my ear. I pressed the transfer button and ran across the room with my notebook to the meeting room, signalling to my boss I wouldn't be long."Fox, hi. Sorry about that. I'm more private now and can hear you better," I advised, slightly out of breath.

"L.J., it's a Friday night. I know this Indian restaurant near my hotel, I go there a lot. Great food, nice staff, no alcohol is served there, though. Do you drink?"

"Do I drink?" I laughed loudly down the phone at him."Save water, drink vodka," I joked.

"You're a vodka drinker?" He sounded surprised."I would have placed you as a red wine drinker."

"I like anything. Red wine's one of my favourites but it gets me into trouble." I closed my eyes and had a few flashbacks.

"Why does it get you into trouble?" He sounded even more amused.

"I get a bit wild and horny," I explained honestly.

"Good to know; I'll buy a few bottles then." He paused and waited for a response.

"Oh God, I didn't even think, I'll need a hotel; can you recommend somewhere for me? I'll have to book it now." I let his flirting moment go over my head and distracted him. He was a client so I couldn't get involved. I'd be fired, and I needed the commission.

"Yes, I'll email them to you just now. Mine's quite reasonable if you can get a room at short notice." He became more professional."So, I'm interested. What else do you do apart from work there? Like I said, I like to know what type of person I'm dealing with. I have a good reputation in the marketplace." His words were hypnotic; he was so easy to listen to, and I felt like I just had to do as I was asked.

"Do you want the truth, or do you want me to bullsh*t?" I wasn't scared of being myself. If he didn't like it, I guess he'd cancel the meeting on me.

"Always the truth. The truth is best." I could tell he was impressed with my directness.

"I've been separated from my husband for two years, spent most of that time shagging, getting drunk, and having a good time, while trying to hold down a responsible job, pay the bills, and look after my two kids. My hobbies are writing pornographic books about my sex life (one published so far), in hope that I will make loads of money and be able to live in a nice house in a nice area miles away from people. People annoy me. I prefer animals; they can't answer back." I waited for the call to hang up as he went deadly silent in complete surprise or shock that I'd been that honest.

"What's your book called?" I heard him typing away into his computer, searching for it.

"A Year of Tiramisu. I wrote it for my f*ck buddy, but he dumped me; I'm still hurting. It cost me £2,000 to publish it, and he'll never even read it." I felt a sudden lurch in my stomach as I still missed him.

"Ordered. I'll read it tonight and give you my review tomorrow when we meet."

"You've what? You're kidding me?"

"Really. I've just got it off Amazon. Great title. How did you come up with it?" He was eager to know everything about me.

"It's what I stuffed my face with every time I got dumped," I lied. I could hardly explain it had been eaten and licked off my entire body. We both started laughing, but again, my mind drifted back to Fancy Pants.

"Any recent dates or seeing other people?" He was definitely fishing to find out if I was available and single.

"A few days ago, I had a date with a woman for the first time. I thought I might have better luck, but it was a disaster." I shuddered at the memory.

"Are you bisexual?" He took a deep breath; I was clearly turning him on.

"Err, I don't think so. Always thought I'd like the idea of a threesome, but never quite got to that point with a guy to experiment," I teased, and I heard him clear his throat.

"You're a refreshing young lady, and I'm very much looking forward to meeting you. I think we'll work well together." He coughed slightly, his voice changing."Can I add you on LinkedIn?" I was now interested in what he looked like; his voice was sexy as hell so he must be attractive. I got my phone out of my pocket and searched for him, added him, then looked at his small photo. I was immediately added back."Wow, is that you? You're stunning," he complimented me, but I didn't compliment him back.

Fox's photo showed a middle-aged man in reasonably good shape, tall, broad-shouldered, with receding grey hair, and a nice smile. His eyes were blue like mine, and he looked kind. The immediate attraction was not lust; it was character. Compared to Fancy Pants, who might as well have been a Ken doll lookalike, they were total opposites."Fox, I could talk to you all day, but the meeting room's booked, so I'm going to have to go and get back to work. I'll see you tomorrow. Don't forget to send me the hotel details." I acted cool and collected even though my heart was pounding. What the hell was happening? All this from a phone conversation?

"I'll look forward to it, L.J. It's been an eye-opening conversation. You've a unique personality."

"Till tomorrow, Fox." I felt oddly sad that the call was about to end. We both waited for each other to hang up, then he said goodbye and was gone. I stood in a daze for a few minutes and thought about what'd just happened, trying to make sense of it logically. Was he flirting? Was I flirting? How did it all feel so familiar, like we'd always talked to each other? Why was I so turned on by him? Then the phone in the meeting room rang again, startling me from my daydream, and it was the intern.

"Fox again on line two." I stared at the phone thinking that he was about to cancel, and all my thoughts had been incorrect.

"Fox? Did you forget something?" I said, worriedly.

"No, I just wanted to hear your voice again." I could feel him smiling down the phone, then he hung up. I beamed a smile and shook my head, pushing my hair back with my hand.

"Weirdo!" I put the phone on its receiver and walked out of the meeting room with a grin on my face.

"L.J., Fox has just emailed me to say that he's never delt with such a professional, knowledgeable consultant. You're off the hook, but don't be late again," my boss shouted across the room.

"Noted, boss." My smile was even wider as I started researching his company and him, ready to write the presentation and meet this sexy, mysterious fox!

CHAPTER SEVEN

"Bang a Gong (Get it On)" ~ T-Rex

I went to the meeting. I didn't present well—I was too distracted by him. But I got the business, and we had mind-blowing sex after the meal.

At first sight of him, I instantly knew he was my next dirty, filthy-minded, sex slave. He was the most unusual man I'd ever looked at that way, not unattractive, but not a model or my usual type. When his eyes looked at me, they were wicked, on fire, and they burnt through me like Superman X-raying a body. I soon discovered that he could mentally take off my clothes and get me to do things I never thought I was capable of. He was a womaniser, a deviant, a player, and a gentleman when he needed to be; above all, he was a magically, mysterious, complex man whom I couldn't unravel.

We f*cked everywhere: in hotel rooms, cars, fields, public toilets, pubs, at my house, in offices, over desks, in elevators, and in restaurants. We didn't care where; we were like wild animals; we couldn't help ourselves. We had phone sex, video sex, even sex over 'Teams.' I wrote about it, endless new chapters for my second book, and I sent them to him, pushing him to his sexual limits, explaining my fantasies, hypnotizing him with what was to come next, and teasing him in every possible way.

Every time we met, I had a different outfit on to greet him, something for every occasion: the filthy Easter bunny, the Valentine's red bow slut, the dominating policewoman, the human Christmas tree covered in glitter paint, space woman with a fake toy gun, sexy sailor's mistress, the horny devil, and the fairy-tale princess, to name a few. Red lipstick, high heels, sex toys, food, long showers together, everything you could think of, we did it, and we invented a few new things along the way.

A year passed, and I was over Fancy Pants; it didn't matter that he'd found himself a younger woman, or that he didn't want me anymore—I'd accepted it. I'd been so hurt by that I thought I'd never let anyone in again. I'd decided that when I did, that was going to be it, my forever person, the love of my life, so I had to be certain.

Fox and I never discussed feelings. We didn't need to; they were naturally there. We called each other every day. He was supportive, he was kind, and he was my ultimate lover. I had struck gold. He'd got so far in my head that I believed he was my best friend and that this perfect combination of him and I would never end.

I left work and got into my car. I always called Fox on my way home because we were usually travelling around the same time, and even if we weren't I could always reach him. I dialled, and he answered within a few rings."Afternoon, L.J. How's your day been?" He was always happy. I don't know how he did it.

"Sh*t, actually. Total pile of steaming sh*t!" I sighed heavily.

"Work?" he assumed.

"Yeah, I just walked out, told them to stick it up their f*cking ass!"

"Good, they didn't treat you well. What's the plan?" He was supportive but straight into 'fix-me' mode.

"Something new, been offered an interview in veterinary recruitment.

One of the guys from here left and went to work for them. He said it's really good, so I'm in tomorrow at 12.30. The management looks a bit out there, but it's local, and the salary matches, with an immediate start."

"Good girl, that was quick. You don't mess around, do you?" he said proudly.

"No, but I could do with a good f*ck. I need a stress release. Where are you?"

"Naughty girl! I'm travelling up from a client visit in London. We can't get together tonight."

"Fox, can we talk? I know we never get serious, but I have a few things I need to say to you."

"Like what? Everything is fine between us."

"Nothing's wrong. God, I love what we have, don't you?"

"Yes, of course I do. You're perfect, this… we, are perfect."

"It's just, we've been f*cking for over twelve months and we've never talked much about feelings or where this is going?"

"Don't change the dynamics, L.J.," he said coldly. I'd never heard him change his tone in such a way. It was unfamiliar, and I got a chill through my body.

"What do you mean? I'm simply telling you that I like you. Wasn't it already obvious?" I frowned and felt hurt by his lack of empathy.

"Look, L.J., what we have is perfect. I enjoy your company and our time together, but I don't do feelings—my heart is black." He went silent and all I could hear was his car travelling.

"You don't do feelings? So, what has the last twelve months been about?" I said, alarmed.

"Sex. We agreed on having a mutual, sexual, no-strings-attached relationship. You've been the coolest woman I've ever met because you've stuck to that agreement. I've got you over that dickhead, Fancy Pants, or you'd have lost the plot." He was right, he had done that much.

"We've been so incredibly intimate; I've never been so close to another person in my life, not even when I was married." I was thrown off by his different version of us.

"I don't do feelings, L.J., and this is not attractive. You're not a desperate, needy person—you stand alone, just like me." He was even more unemotional and direct now, and I didn't recognise him."We have fun. Do you want to lose that?" He seemed rational and honest, but not the person I'd grown to know.

"Look, Fox. I thought we were going somewhere. I genuinely thought we were in some kind of a relationship." I started to choke up.

"You only have yourself, and I only have myself, L.J. It's the same for every person on the planet. Otherwise, you get let down." I felt pain in his voice and knew there was a reason for this that he wasn't clearly explaining.

"So, what if I said I loved you?" I decided to be brave and just get it out into the universe. He took a long time to answer me—it was an uncomfortable silence.

"I can never love you," he said coldly. I pulled the car over and parked outside my house. What I had to lose at that point was more important to me than my happy ever after, but I was now in a massive internal battle between my head and my heart.

"I need a few days to think about this if that's okay? My head's a bit f*cked from this conversation." I held it together, trying not to let him hear me cry.

"Take as as you need," he said with no emotion and hung up.

CHAPTER EIGHT

"Teardrops from My Eyes" ~ Ruth Brown

Propping my head up at my desk with one hand, I looked miserable, pale, and tired; the endless long nights of drinking and writing my second book were catching up with me. The last conversation with Fox had drained so much of my self-worth that I wasn't sure I'd ever fully recover. I was so in love and broken.

I replied to a few work emails before dragging myself slowly out of my seat to make my morning coffee. I heard the rain beating down outside and hitting the window, making tapping sounds on the glass like my long nails typing too fast on a keyboard."Shush," I begged pathetically, holding my head with both hands.

I took two headache tablets for the incessant pain that throbbed in my brain. Holding my head with one hand and my drink in the other, my hand shook uncontrollably on its way toward my dry mouth. The familiar sickly feeling deep in my stomach had kicked in as my hangover slowly worsened, and I wished I could be at home under my duvet, fast asleep. My dreams were a better reality than my life right now.

My phone rang in my jeans pocket, startling me, causing me to spill coffee on the floor and down my leg. I cursed. It was Fox. Rolling my eyes, I reluctantly answered. I really couldn't be bothered with his critical parenting opinions on how I was supposed to be living my life, which he frequently forced upon me.

"Morning, L.J.," he sighed down the phone,"How are you today, Ugly?"

"Take a look in the mirror at yourself, you cheeky ass!" I fired a response right back at him, already losing interest in the conversation.

"Hungover?" he observed from my lack of enthusiasm for a conversation with him.

"I was writing our book until 4am, then I got up for work at 6am. I'm just tired." I partly lied but didn't care. Drinking every night was now a habit, and not an excuse for helping me be more creative. Even when I wasn't writing, I was drinking because I felt so lonely; the bottle had become my worst nightmare, yet my most welcoming friend.

Honesty wasn't something I thought he deserved any more, and I didn't want him to know that he'd had such a massive impact on my mental health, or that I'd lost control because of him.

"What does it matter anyway? We aren't together, are we? You explained that to me quite clearly," I snapped, then bit my lip to stop myself from crying in anger and frustration. The rejection had deeply affected me and my confidence. His lack of empathy toward me was unnerving. I still couldn't wrap my head around any of it.

I didn't want him in the same way that I had before. The love and respect I'd had for him was spoiled; it felt dirty and cheap. My feelings toward him had become obsessive and distorted because of it, and worst of all, the craving for sex, and for someone I couldn't have. History was repeating itself! It was just like Fancy Pants all over again.

"Fox, I have five candidates to interview. I need to get back to work, unless you want to listen to me talk about anal gland removals all morning?" I tried to change the subject to avoid getting into matters any deeper, while thinking of a few things I could quite happily remove from his body without sedation.

"L.J., don't be like this, it doesn't suit you. I thought we agreed to be friends?" I paused for a long time, knowing I couldn't handle the conversation much longer without swearing down the phone that he was a royal knobhead and listing all the reasons why in an intensely unpleasant way.

"Look, I need to go," I said assertively but terrified of hanging up on him. I had no idea what telling him 'no' would do.

"Okay, but please call me if you need anything. I won't change my number or block you. I'm still here for you, always," he said in a soft, loving voice, which completely threw me."It's the big 'four-o' in a few weeks, isn't it?" He surprised me by remembering my birthday."I've already got you a little something. It's nothing much, but I wanted you to have something unique."

I gasped down the phone in surprise."You remembered? You didn't have to get me anything," I said, blushing, trying not to give away too much of my real reaction over the phone.

"Can we meet for a coffee that day?" he asked, making my head dizzy with emotion.

"I'll think about it," I said, confused.

"Maybe we could have a rendezvous?" he continued, knowing my weakness.

"Fox, how about you go f*ck yourself?" I said angrily and hung up. People's heads in the office rose from their desks in disgust. What game was he playing with me? Why did he not just disappear and let me live my life?

I rushed to the bathroom, my heart pounding. Running the cold tap, I washed my face in cold water to stop myself being sick. Staring at my reflection in the mirror, I fell deep into thought. I'd never loved a man so much and hated him at the same time. I'd realised I didn't know anything about him. Who was he? I didn't know what I was supposed to think or feel, or even how I'd get through such a complicated mess in my head.

All I knew was that I was desperately, unhealthily, in love, and the only thing stopping me from going insane was pouring my heart out into the publication of my second book while listening to Sinatra and crying myself to sleep with a bottle of wine every night.

Dragging myself back to my desk, I sat down and faced the window. The rain had stopped, and I stared out at the clouds passing by, my mind processing things at a million miles an hour but getting nowhere. I was gladly distracted by my laptop as it made a 'ping' sound to notify me of a new email. Putting my glasses on, I opened it, and it was from my publisher, a forwarded message saying, 'Morning, L.J., I presume this is for you…'

The message read"Hi, I'm trying to reach L.J. Brown. We met a year ago and lost contact. I know you're her publisher. Can you please forward her my email and mobile number? Tell her it's Mr Belfast—she'll understand." Reading the message, I gasped, then chuckled. What a surprise! An incredible one-night stand from a year ago. One fateful night at the meat awards when a beautiful man saved me from having a fight with a giant teddy bear.

I replied to my publisher with, 'Oh my God, yes, I know who he is. Thank you for forwarding this to me.' In utter disbelief, I closed my eyes and thought back to a year ago, and an unexpected night of raw passion with Mr Belfast, the sexy Irish stranger.

CHAPTER NINE

"Cry to Me" ~ Solomon Burke

One year earlier, a week after sleeping with Fox for the first time, life had become quite hectic. Splitting my time between working full-time, my children, and writing was becoming almost unbearable, so when I got the chance to kick back, I welcomed it with open arms.

I'd been invited by a client to a networking event in London —a ball gown and black-tie event. I was more than happy to spend my Friday night child-free, drinking champagne, and dancing until late, while looking like a princess. The butcher awards happened every few years to celebrate the UK and Ireland's best. I couldn't help but think that the room would be filled with the finest pork pie and sausage makers of all time and had no idea how I'd keep a straight face and not crack inappropriate jokes all evening.

Arriving at the hotel, I reached for my car parking ticket and went through the barriers to find a free space. The hotel looked like it needed to be bulldozed. I rolled my eyes, put on my shades, and took a deep breath."For f*ck's sake, another epically sh*t hotel. Well done, boss," I said to myself, imagining that I might actually see the imprint of the last person murdered in my hotel room this time.

Checking in, I glanced around to find signs for the bar, where I practically ran to order a large glass of wine. I looked around the room. The high ceiling was filled with cracks and damp patches that had dried out and been left stained, and the walls were dated with dark depressing wallpaper peeling off. The hotel was in desperate need of a makeover, and I hoped that my hotel bed wouldn't fall through the floor.

"Many people staying here for the awards?" I asked, pulling out a bar stool and gulping my wine down.

"The awards? Have you got the right hotel?" The bartender looked confused, scratching his head.

"Never mind," I replied politely. I held my head in my hands and glanced down at my phone. I had four missed calls from Fox and a few texts I hadn't replied to. I called him back excitedly."Four calls, Fox. Are you becoming my stalker?" I said sarcastically down the phone.

"L.J., I know what your driving's like; I was just making sure you'd not driven into the back end of a bus. Are you at your hotel yet?" He sounded genuinely happy to have finally reached me. I could tell he was so into me, but I wasn't there yet. It was early days, and I still had Fancy Pants on my mind.

"I got lost five times." I laughed down the phone and drank more wine. He had cheered me up already, teasing me about my navigational skills."So, I've got a hotel room. Come stay the night with me?" I said seductively, hoping for him to say yes.

"I've got a big hardon for you, L.J., but I'm miles away and have plans tonight," he said regretfully.

"Oh, really? What are you doing?" I quizzed, disappointed.

"It's just a work thing. I can't get out of it." He sounded off guard, and I frowned.

"Okay, who with? And is it anything fun?" He went quiet and didn't answer. Instead, he changed the subject."Why are you not telling me?" I asked in a matter-of-fact way, feeling confused.

"Look, L.J., I have to go. Just about to go into a meeting." He lowered his tone and hung up.

"Okay, speak later," I said, with no one there at the end of the phone to hear it. How rude, I thought. What the heck was all that about? I drank my wine and ordered a bottle for the room.

Thanking the bartender, I took the wine and my case to the old-fashioned elevator, then made a crucifix sign across my chest, closed my eyes, and took the elevator to level ten. Finding my key, I heard the phone ring again—it was my boss. Holding the phone to my ear with my shoulder, I awkwardly struggled to get into the room with a case and wine bottle.

"You got there okay, L.J.? What's the room like?" he boomed with authority down the phone at me.

I looked around the room. It had twin beds, a worn carpet, and a propped-up desk with a cracked mirror."It... lovely," I lied, popping my head into the bathroom and rolling my eyes. What an absolute sh*thole, I thought, smelling the sheets to make sure they'd been recently washed.

"Good, I wanted you to have the best." I pulled a face in disbelief and looked around for a glass, taking it to the bathroom and washing it before drinking my wine out of it."Make sure you hand out business cards and come back with new clients. I haven't put you in a nice hotel for nothing, L.J." I put him on speaker and stuck my tongue out at him.

"On it, boss. See you tomorrow afternoon." What a loser, I thought. I'm so going to leave his crappy company just as soon as I can.

Glancing at my phone, I thought I'd better reply to my messages. Reading one of them made me freeze in shock. I felt like I'd been hit with a ton of bricks. It read,"Look, I've met someone, she's perfect. For the first time in my life, I don't want to mess around, so I'm texting you to say we can't talk any more, okay? We need to drop all contact. I respect her too much. Take care, and good luck with the books. Fancy Pants x"

I stared at it for a few minutes before replying."I'm really happy for you," I lied, starting to cry."I'll delete your number. Very best of luck too x" I stared into my glass and looked at his handsome profile picture on my phone one last time before deleting his contact details and removing him from my recent calls. I was never going to be with him, and I knew that now, but it hurt so much to know he was happy, and I wasn't, without him.

"Two men in ten minutes have rejected me. World record!" I said to myself. I flung myself onto the bed and stared into space for a while before dragging myself into the shower to get ready, taking the wine in with me. My motivation for looking good seemed pretty pointless because I felt so flat. I slipped my elegant dress over my head; it would have to do the work for me tonight. I styled my hair and put a small amount of make-up on to look respectable.

I got to the venue in a taxi, stepping out carefully, holding my beautiful light green gown up off the ground. I was dressed impeccably, wearing pearls and white stiletto heels. I handed my ticket to reception and glided my way confidently along the hallway toward the bar to order a drink.

"A very large glass of Merlot, please," I asked firmly, reaching into my purse for my card. As I looked up, a man sat drinking at the other side of the bar caught my eye. He was smiling at me and staring, it felt like I had been hit with a bolt of lightning, maybe the universe had just sifted, it was like my body had just merged with his, with just one look into his eyes. What an incredible unexpected feeling. The handsome stranger was in a black tie and looked like he was as late as me and didn't care either. He nodded and smiled even wider, raising his glass to me.

"The drink's on the gentleman at the bar," the bartender said in a thick Brummie accent, making it a completely unromantic moment. I looked at him confused, then looked back to communicate with the stranger to say thank you, but he was gone.

"Cheers!" I raised my glass to the empty seat, wondering where he'd gone, why he bought me the drink, and really affected by the eye contact we'd had.

I walked to the room and checked the seating list, running my fingers down a sea of names until I found mine right at the back. That was just perfect. I felt a sense of relief. If things got too bad, I could easily exit. I picked my dress up, so it didn't get caught in my heels, and switched into professional mode. I had to get some contacts tonight.

When I entered, the room was dark, apart from the dazzling lights on the stage and candles on the tables. I found my table and looked for my name before taking my seat. I glanced around at everyone, all strangers, and smiled nervously.

A man and woman to the right of me politely introduced themselves."Welcome to the awards. What butchers do you work for?" A red-faced man bursting out of his suit leaned over the table to shake my hand, squeezing it too hard.

"I don't work for a butcher, and I'm not a butcher. In fact, I don't like pies that much at all. I work for a recruitment agency that specialises in your industry. I was invited by a client." I blushed, hoping he wouldn't roll his eyes. Not many people liked recruiters at the best of times, and my client hadn't put me on his table, obviously for that very reason.

"Hello, it's nice to meet you. We're up for the 'Best Butcher in the UK' award tonight." He sniffed at me, looking down his nose.

"Oh sh*t, I mean, oh, bollocks, well, good for you. Keep making pies!" I sat in my seat and glugged the wine down. This was going to be a long and painful night of dullness.

I sat trying to make polite conversation, steadily getting more and more drunk, eating tiny portions of cuisine and clapping for awards I had no interest in. It seemed to go on forever, and once the show was over, I got out of my seat and tried to make a quick exit for the toilets before the endless queues began.

My arm was grabbed gently as I squeezed between the tables trying not to get my dress caught. I turned, and it was the stranger from the bar."I've been watching you all night. You're stunning, even when you're bored." He smiled at me and held my hand to kiss it."Can I buy you another drink?" he shouted over the DJ announcing that the dance floor was open. His accent was Irish.

"Sure, I'll meet you at the bar. I need to visit the little girls' room," I shouted into his ear over the deafening music.

"Fantastic, I'll see you at the bar." He winked and walked away backwards, watching me walk across the busy room, both of us smiling like teenagers—both of us obviously also drunk.

"Sexy Irish man," I shouted, as he walked away from me."If I can't find you and we bump into each other again before the end of the night, we'll go back to the hotel together," I said confidently.

"It's a deal." He looked at me surprised but happy.

My ears were ringing, and my head was a little dizzy. Looking at myself in the mirror, I re-applied my make-up and squirted myself with perfume. I tried to talk some sense into my reflection."I want to sleep with him. L.J., you'll not regret it in the morning. Oh, God, I'm drunk!"

I walked back into the venue. People were falling about and laughing around me, drunken and merry. I loved to see people happy. I smiled and made my way to the bar. Pushing the double doors open, I looked out into a sea of people and what seemed to be giant teddy bears. I rubbed my eyes in disbelief. Had someone put LSD in my drink? I slowly walked to the bar and propped myself against it. Ordering a drink, I looked around for the handsome stranger, who was nowhere in sight.

It was surreal, a mixture of elegant ball gowns and smart black tie, mixed with man-sized Sonic hedgehogs and Mario brothers. Surely I was high?"Has my drink been spiked, or is that Barney the dog?" I pulled a confused, drunk face at the bartender.

"Ha. No, you're not seeing things. One of the venues had a problem with their electrics, so they got moved into the same bar area. People are here from all over the world for this; it's called 'Confuzzled'. It's a 'furry convention'."

"I'm Confuzzled." I snorted a laugh out loud and paid for my drink. I looked around with my mouth open. This was crazy to observe. Every animal you could think of was walking around the bar with cocktails and wine glasses in their hands. Something that resembled Paddington Bear walked over to the bar, stood right next to me, and waved his big hand.

I waved back awkwardly."Are you not hot in that outfit?" I shouted over the noise and smiled, amused."Did you know that a wise bear always keeps his marmalade sandwiches in his hat, in case of emergencies?" I continued, mocking him. He took his giant hand off to pay for his drink, then politely gave me the finger. I turned back to the bartender and we both laughed.

I then got a tap on the shoulder. I put my hands in the air thinking Paddington had come over to shout some abuse."For the love of Christ, F*CK OFF, you big hairy freakshow!" I had myself ready for a drunken verbal dispute.

"Want to get out of here?" a thick northern Irish accent said firmly. I felt a warm hand in mine and opened one eye, then two, slightly scared of what I might see next when I turned around. My perfect stranger had tracked me down.

"It's you," I gasped thankfully."Oh, yes, pleaaaase." I pulled myself off the seat and stumbled. Standing closer to him now I smelled his aftershave and cleared my throat nervously.

"I've got you, don't worry. And yes, before you ask, I'm freaked out too, but it's slightly hilarious, don't you think?" He guided me to the exit of the hotel, flagged a taxi, and helped me in."To the airport," he instructed the taxi driver and looked back at me next to him in the back seat.

"Are we getting on a plane, because I have serious helicopter head already." I was seeing double and feeling a little sick.

"No planes today," he laughed."God, you're beautiful," he said, holding my face with his hand. He was so gentle and manly."You're so beautiful," he repeated as he pushed my hair away from my face and smiled.

"So are you, I think, I can see your twin right now, and I could've totally pulled Paddington Bear back there, but I guess you'll have to do," I teased, my eyes lit up by him. He smelt so intoxicating and felt so familiar, it was like I'd met him before. I was completely comfortable, and it felt natural almost immediately.

"Look at the state o' you," he said in his sexy Irish twang. He took off his jacket and wrapped it around me."Let's sober you up and get coffee somewhere quiet. I want to know all about you."

"What do you want to know?" I rested my head on the back seat and looked into his eyes.

Leaning to face each other, I closed my eyes, and he kissed me. It was the most intense kiss of my life, like our mouths were supposed to fit together. My heart beat so fast I thought I was about to have a heart attack. It was instant lust and connection just like in the bar, like a thunderbolt or bomb had gone off inside me.

"Can't we just go to your room? I'm horny," I said eagerly, desperate to see how this would work in the bedroom, never having had explosive chemistry this intense before.

"No. Coffee. I want to have the pleasure of having a conversation if that's okay?" I was startled that he was so hot and such a gentleman. We pulled up and got out of the taxi at a hotel much posher than mine, and I felt excited to be somewhere nice for a change. He supported me with his hand and guided me through the hotel lobby toward a bar and restaurant area that didn't look far from closing. I looked around and saw it was on the same floor as a casino.

"Where have you brought me?" My jaw dropped at how exciting it all looked."Let's play, let's play. I'm going to win so much money," I said, jumping up and down like a schoolgirl in a sweet shop.

"We're near the airport. I have the penthouse apartment," he replied with a grin, laughing at my behaviour.

"I feel like I'm in Pretty Woman," I exclaimed, as he guided me to the nearest available table and got the waiter's attention.

"How do you take your coffee?" he asked as the waiter approached the table.

"White, two sugars, strong." I thanked him as he paid.

"So, tell me all about you." He poured milk into my coffee and stirred in sugar.

"Can't we just go to bed?" I looked at him longingly, thinking, after all, this is just a shag, right? I've been here a few too many times.

"No, have some respect for yourself. I've not even asked that of you," he replied carefully, trying not to insult me.

"What do you mean? You're a man. All they do is use women for sex." I slumped in my chair and looked bored.

"Not all men are like that. I saw you at the bar and just had to meet you. That's as far as I've got in my head, and now here we are having coffee." He became slightly shy around me.

"But you're so handsome, you must get so much attention?" I looked at him, confused.

"Believe me, I'm attracted to you, but I want you to feel respected. I don't do this as often as you might think. I'm quite selective." He sat and talked to me for what seemed forever, slowly sobering me up and making sure I was okay. I told him about Fancy Pants and writing a book about it. He looked at the evidence I'd provided on my phone and shook his head in amusement."I can't believe I'm sitting here with an author."

"It's out in a few weeks." I yawned as I spoke, my hangover kicking in.

"Well, I'm impressed. It's not every day you meet a published author in the flesh." He beamed at me, his perfect teeth showing. He rubbed his fingers through his thick pointed beard."Do you want me to call you a cab, get you back to your hotel? It's late." He looked at his watch, concerned, and pulled me toward him, noticing I was still cold.

"Can I not just sleep here?" I put my head down on the table and pulled his jacket over my head; it instantly filled me with his scent."I'm going to have nightmares about giant teddy bears if I sleep alone." I snorted out a laugh but wasn't joking.

"Okay, come on then, but I think you do need some sleep." He poked his head under his jacket and grinned at me, shaking his head. We walked to the elevator where I cuddled into him, and we kissed all the way until we reached the top floor. He tasted of coffee and Jack Daniel's, and I didn't want to take my lips away from his.

"Wow," I said when he opened the hotel room door, and I saw the luxury bedroom in front of me."It's bigger than the bar we've just sat in," I bellowed in amazement.

"It was on the company," he said, as if it wasn't all that important. I grabbed his hand and pulled him across the room.

"Gosh, they must sell a lot of pies." I giggled and pushed my head into his chest, playfully.

"Look, you have a balcony overlooking the airport!" I opened the doors and walked out to look at the sky and how high up we were."Top floor. This is so cool." I squeezed his hand and pulled him near me, pointing to everything that amazed me. He turned me around and looked at me, not really knowing what we were going to do next, just lost in the moment.

"I make a lot of noise when I'm having sex." I brushed back his thick, dark hair, and ran my finger over his lip, slowly unfastening his belt with my other hand, not taking my eyes off him. I placed my hand down his pants to feel how hard he was."F*ck me!" I said with utter surprise."Have you packed an elephant down there?"

"I have to see this!" I said in delight. I pushed his pants down to the floor and backed away from him, waving my finger."Err, absolutely no way that's going to fit inside me." I put both hands to my face and peeked through them at him. We both started to laugh, then launched into a passionate kiss."Seriously, though," I said into his mouth,"What is it with Irish men and big dicks?"

"Guinness." He smiled into my mouth and picked me up in his arms."It's past your bedtime, beautiful Yorkshire writer. Let me get you to sleep."

"Have you ever been in love before?" he asked. I suddenly felt completely sober as I felt things I'd never felt before and didn't understand them.

"I don't really know if I have or not. I know I've been hurt by guys, so I must've cared enough," I said sadly."I have to admit to you, I'm getting over the guy I wrote the book about, and I've been seeing someone new for a week. I guess I don't know what I'm doing or how I feel, and he's much older. I'm a bit confused with my feelings toward 'love'." We both fell silent.

"I've been where you are right now. I don't think you're doing anything wrong. You're technically single." He pulled his t-shirt over his head to reveal his toned body, covered in thick, jet-black hair, and got into bed, pulling the sheets back for me, and reaching out his hand."Come on, talk to me about it. Get it all out." He turned to face me, paying me his full attention.

"Okay… well, I was married for a long time. Ten years. I had a terrible marriage; he was a drunk who used to belittle me, swear at me, and finally he cheated, so I left him. Then, a few months later, I met this guy through online dating. He lit me up like a Christmas tree, and

I'm scared I'll never have that again, the spark and passion. He's met someone else, and I was dropped in a heartbeat." I gave a big sigh, my heart squeezed painfully at the thought of them both together, happy. But then I thought about how tonight I'd had such a massive spark with the man lying next to me, so perhaps all was not lost.

"Rejection can sometimes be seen as God's protection. Maybe you've had a lucky escape." He stroked my leg lightly."If it's meant to be, he'll come back to you somehow. You can't beat yourself up; it's just life. This happens to so many of us." He sounded like he was talking from experience.

"You're right, but I think I better finish it with Fox in the morning. I'm in bed with another man, so it's clearly not right." I started to worry about what I was going to say to him. I couldn't tell him the truth; he'd be so disappointed in me.

"I'd say that's the right thing to do, yes." He brushed my hair away from my eyes and wiped away my tears."Now, shall we relax and enjoy ourselves?" he asked, with a wild smile.

"Nope, I think I'll go call that cab." I was jesting, but he almost believed me.

"You're a wild one, you are," he said, kissing my forehead.

"I'm only doing this because I like your Irish accent, and I like Guinness." I chuckled and laid beside him, pulling the covers up to look at his erection again."Jesus Christ on a bike, I'll never walk again. It's seriously not going to fit. I thought leprechauns were supposed to be small!" I pulled the covers over our heads and giggled, getting on top of him to kiss him playfully, my head spinning still from too much wine.

"Will you write about what happens tonight?" He held my face and kissed me softly.

"Do you want me to?" I sounded surprised, pulling myself away from his lips.

"Yes, I want you to write about all our nights," he said without thinking, and I looked at him sideways.

"I have a big imagination; does that scare you?" I tested him, and he looked at me reluctantly.

"Let's go back out onto the balcony," I ordered him, slipping out of my dress.

"What, naked? People might see us!" He was stunned by my request.

"F*cking high up is on my to-do list, and I thought you were taking me on a plane tonight," I said wickedly, pulling him out of the bed."I'll bend over the balcony, and you take me from behind." I directed him assertively, now completely turned on.

It was cold, and my nipples became hard like bullets. My body covered itself in goosebumps, and my breath quickened as I watched myself exhale into the cold night sky. He teased me with his fingers slowly, then pushed his fingers in and tickled my g-spot until I moaned.

"I only ever got as far as coffee in my head, you know." He kissed my ear and bit it gently. I leaned into him in acknowledgment of his respect for me. He kissed my back and slowly pushed himself inside me. My eyes closed together tightly. He filled me like no one ever had and it felt delightful, yet strange, a little like losing my virginity all over again. Slowly, he picked up rhythm and pulled me to an upright position still locked inside me, holding onto my breasts, squeezing them tightly, and biting my neck.

I saw people walking around outside like little ants on the floor. It felt so deviant and sexy, but so right."Oh, God, I'm going to cum," I screamed, my body building and breath quickening. A plane was taking off from the airport, and I watched it while it roared into the night sky in front of me and giggled to myself whilst moaning in pleasure.

He pushed my head to one side and whispered into my ear,"Now you can scream as much as you want." He turned me around, lifted me up against the edge, and pounded into me. I watched his cock going in and out of me while falling apart, him trying to support me so I didn't fall over the edge. I came everywhere, soaking us both, making the most noise I've ever made, and thanks to the screech of the plane taking off, no one could have heard but us. It was so intense and so hot, I wanted more instantly. Every part of my body felt like it had been switched on to full voltage. I was so alive.

"Well, the pilot got a good view!" I said out of breath, pulling my head back up to watch the plane fly away. Stars filled the night sky and reflected in his eyes as he stood there out of breath in front of me. He was so handsome, and naughty, yet so perfectly kind. What had I just found? My equal?"I'm cold," I said, shivering, hugging myself, my thoughts racing about what'd just happened.

"You won't be in a minute." He put me back on the floor securely and kissed me passionately. My lips tingled with the rush of endorphins coursing through me. He picked me up again, which took me by surprise, then put me over his shoulder. I yelped.

"I'll throw up on you," I screamed with laugher.

"You need some new material for your book?" he jested, placing me gently on the bed, then turning back to shut the balcony doors. I watched his beautiful silhouette in the moonlight, and the shadow of his erection hit the bed as he walked back toward me."Again?" he asked, getting into bed.

"If you insist!" I put my hand over my mouth, giggling, looking into his eyes that were now on fire with lust. I knew I'd really turned him on, and I was turned on too."What do you want to do? I'm a bit of a sexpert." I tried to intimidate him but realised the coin had just flipped.

He leaned in to kiss me and whispered softly into my ear,"F*cking everything!"

"Promise me we'll meet again?"

"I promise." He kissed me and turned out the light.

CHAPTER TEN

"Castles Made of Sand" ~ Jimi Hendrix

Fox had called nearly every day and explained his point of view to me over and over in a desperate attempt to console me and make me feel secure with him again. I'd admitted to him that I was in love with him and that I couldn't stop it, no matter how hard I tried, but I was now in constant conflict. This wasn't how I expected to fall in love, and I didn't feel comfortable. I was insanely in love with an emotionally unavailable man.

I tried to find reasons to destroy it and ways to pull away from him, but it felt like we were locked together, and I couldn't escape. I couldn't run away from my feelings, and it seemed hopeless to even try.

He planned to spend my birthday with me, and I was delighted that he wanted to. This would be the first time since we split up a month ago that we were going to be together again. I was a mixture of emotional delight and apprehension. I could hardly contain my feelings, and I was super horny.

"Happy Birthday, L.J.!" My mum phoned and started singing to me like I was twelve years old again."Forty, gosh; I feel so old. I remember bringing you home from the hospital. Everyone loved you. What a beautiful, happy baby you were," she sighed lovingly.

"Yeah, what happened to me?" I laughed loudly, pulling her leg."It's just a number, Mum." I didn't feel or think I looked forty years old. I was dashing around with the phone to my ear, putting candles out everywhere and scattering rose petals on the bed, ready for Fox to arrive. I was so excited about spending my birthday with him, and especially having amazing sex again.

"So, you're spending the day with your new man, then? I hope he gets you something nice and spoils you," she said, not sounding very convinced. She didn't seem to like him much and hadn't even met him yet."He's too old for you, L.J. I'm not really comfortable with this," she scolded.

"Mum, I'm happy, and I'm in love—I think. At least it's not Fancy Pants I'm spending the weekend with!" I said with bitter reflection.

"Filthy, horrible, using bastard," she cursed."Don't you ever speak to him again, will you, or I'll be so cross." She huffed and tutted in disgust at the thought of him.

"In the past, Mum. He's toast," I said convincingly."Now, let the birthday girl get ready. I love you, Mum. Thank you for having me," I said sweetly, making sounds of kisses down the phone at her. She started to cry. As I hung up, the phone immediately rang again; it was my best friend.

"Wello, Wusan," I screamed down the phone in delight. We'd had pet names for each other since we were young.

"Happy birthday, Darling. Are you all set?" She knew what my birthday plans were and what I was preparing for Fox.

"Yes, just dashing around the house trying to get ready for him. He's not text me yet, so I imagine he'll just turn up," I said excitedly.

"Make sure you try that new sex position I was telling you about," she insisted."It will blow your f*cking head off!" We both laughed down the phone like silly schoolgirls.

"I can't wait. I've told him all about it already. He's up for it. Wants me to do a handstand against the wall and go down on me too. I better stay reasonably sober."

"Make sure you don't kick him in the face on the way down." She burst into laughter and then wished me luck."I'm still not sure he's telling you the truth. Just be careful, okay? I know you love him, but I'm not convinced that he's entirely genuine." She sounded concerned while trying to do her best to be happy for me.

"It's going to be fine. He won't let me down. Who would do a thing like that on someone's birthday?" I dismissed the possibility, reassuring her, and told her I'd call her in the morning with all the gory details.

I rushed around my immaculate house, lit the candles, plated up the strawberries and cream and put the champagne on ice, then hushed the cats out of the house because of his allergies to them. I checked my make-up in the mirror; it was perfect. Bright red lipstick, lush hair, and dressed in expensive lace bra, panties, and stockings, with bright red shoes to match my lips. I felt amazing, and I couldn't wait to be with him, and for him to be inside me again, his skin on mine.

I looked at my phone and still no message or calls from him. I paced up and down the room then decided to hit the call button. He hung up immediately. Perhaps he was driving, so I decided to send him a text."Birthday girl here… I'm ready for you! Looking sexy and feeling f*cking horny. Love L.J. x"

Within minutes I got a message back saying, "I'm sorry, something's come up. I feel awful, but I can't make it." I walked to the sofa and slumped down, reading back the message that didn't even contain a kiss, then quickly replying to his text in disbelief.

"Is this a joke? Ha ha, very funny!" I replied, smiling, and shaking my head.

"No, I'm sorry. I'll make it up to you," he responded swiftly.

WHAT? IT'S MY FORTIETH BIRTHDAY! I've cancelled all my plans with family to be with you. Now I'm going to be alone!" I texted in capitals, shouting at him.

"I'm sorry, I have something that I have to deal with. I'll call you later. I still have your gift." I thought of a few things he could do with his gift that were unpleasant, then the shock kicked in. He really wasn't coming.

"Do you know what, Fox? Shove your f*cking gift right up your ass. I can't believe this; I've gone to so much effort. We are so done!" I bit my lip and screwed my face up.

"L.J., I have a reason. Let me explain later. STOP BEING A CHILD. It's not all about you, you know," he replied in capitals, shouting back.

In complete anger and disappointment, I kicked off my heels, walked into the kitchen, and popped open the champagne bottle, letting it spill over. Drinking out of the bottle, I quickly started to strip off my underwear and scatter it around in careless frustration. Finally, I slid down the wall onto the floor, determined to sit there and finish the bottle.

More relaxed from the alcohol, I tilted my head to one side and selected some music to listen to. "Siri, play how to fix a broken heart," I demanded pathetically.

"Now playing How to Fix a Broken Heart, by Guy Winch," it replied promptly.

"Who the f*ck's Guy Winch?" I protested, thinking of something else to select when a voice boomed out of my speakers.

"At some point in our lives almost every one of us will have our heart broken." I was caught off guard. It wasn't a song, but in my drunken state I started to hang off every word he was saying in astonishment.

"One of my patients planned her wedding when she was in middle school: she would meet her future husband by age 27, get engaged a year later, and get married a year after that. However, when she actually turned 27, she didn't find a husband; she found a lump in her breast and went through harsh chemotherapy and painful surgeries. Just as she was ready to jump back into the dating world, she found a lump in her other breast and had to do it all over again." Feeling drunk, I laughed uncomfortably at her situation, and began to cry at the same time, thinking how pathetic I was for only being stood up, and how minor all this was in the big scheme of things.

He described how soon afterward, she'd started dating, and fell in love. Then, on the night she'd expected him to propose, he broke up with her. I pulled myself up to pay more attention to what I was listening to and asked Siri to turn up the volume.

He shared how after five months, her heart was still very much broken, but she couldn't understand why. Why would a woman strong and determined enough to get through four years of cancer treatment be unable to marshal the same emotional resources to deal with her heartbreak? My eyes grew large as I understood how I'd felt about Fancy Pants, and now it looked like the pattern was repeating with Fox. What was wrong with me? I'm a strong woman too!

I listened to his intelligent words echo around my kitchen."Why do the same coping mechanisms that get us through all kinds of life challenges fail us so badly when our hearts get broken?"

I gasped in recognition of my situation."It's me. This is me!" I shouted and began pacing up and down the room naked, kicking balloons out of the way.

He continued to explain that despite the man caring for her, he simply wasn't in love with her. I sighed in recognition; just like Fox, I thought, bursting into tears again, and thinking about opening another bottle. If he loved me, he would've been here today. Nothing would've stopped him."Why is love so blind?" I screamed in pain.

He offered advice on how to fix a broken heart, saying that we have to re-establish who we are and what our life is about, filling the void in our social lives and activities. He warned that,"None of it will do any good if you're idealising your ex and how he was right or wrong for you. Indulging thoughts that still give them a starring role in the next chapter of your life, when they shouldn't even be an extra."

I sat back and contemplated how much effort I'd put into writing two books for two men who literally didn't give a flying f*ck about me. I refused to be a victim. Instead, I felt anger and determination to start to move away from this behaviour.

"If you refuse to be misled by your mind and you take steps to heal, you can significantly minimise your suffering. You'll be more present with your friends and more engaged with your family." I nodded in acknowledgement. I knew I'd been all-consumed and distant from everyone since becoming involved with Fox, and this realisation hit me quite hard, as people who really cared had started walking away from me.

"If you're hurting, know this: it's a battle in your own mind, and you have to be diligent to win, but you do have weapons. You can fight, and you will heal."

I clapped my hands together in applause."Pull yourself back together, L.J.," I told myself out loud."This is absolutely his loss." I blew out the candles one by one, singing happy birthday to myself, then ran upstairs. I grabbed my gym kit and placed my swimming clothes into a sports bag."If it's a fight I'm going to have with myself, I know I'll never let myself lose," I said through gritted teeth. Feeling motivated, but needing to process the pain, I knew I needed to get my aggression out at the gym; it was the only way I knew how.

Going back downstairs, I stopped in my tracks. I picked up my heels and put them back on, placing my gym bag on the floor. I stood on one of the balloons and said aggressively,"F*ck you, Fox!" and popped it loudly with my heel, then got a taste for it and stamped on them all."F*cking twat, bastard, sh*tty asshole!" The balloons popped one by one, leaving a mess all over my kitchen floor."No one stands L.J. up!" I said with conviction, kicking off my heels and replacing them with trainers. Heading for the door, I looked back at the romantic mess I'd left behind."Happy f*cking birthday, L.J.," I said with a heavy sigh.

CHAPTER ELEVEN

"Stood Up" ~ Ricky Nelson

Checking into the gym, I scanned my card, grabbed my towel, and headed toward the changing rooms. I found a cubical and pulled the curtain shut. Taking my clothes off slowly, I stared at myself in the mirror. My hair fell down over my breasts and the overhead light reflected off my belly button ring. My face looked thin and drawn, and the contours of my body looked perfectly womanly. What was wrong with me, for him to not want me?

I took a deep breath and reached for my bag, pulling out the second bottle of champagne. I popped the cork, not caring if anyone would hear, then drank out of the bottle, my eyes still fixated on my reflection. Am I losing my looks? Putting on weight? Or perhaps just too old for him now? I frowned at my reflection, then turned away.

I reached for my phone and started to take seductive photos of myself, making sure the mirror caught part of the image, checking, and deleting them until I got the perfect shot. 'Drinking our champagne at the gym.' I sent the image and text to Fox, then slumped down on the seat in the changing room, drinking more from the bottle and waiting for a response.

"I wanted to be there. You look amazing." A text came almost immediately, which surprised me.

"Well, it's absolutely your loss. I'm drunk and about to get into a bikini," I quickly replied.

"Have a good time. I have to go." He vanished yet again.

Dragging myself up, trying not to cry, I got dressed into my bikini, gathered my things, and headed toward a locker, still drinking out of the bottle."You know you're not supposed to drink in the gym," an older woman with a smart mouth snapped at me.

"It's my birthday," I snapped back,"and I've just been stood up, so I'll do whatever I please!" I continued to make eye contact as my face reddened in anger. She knew not to say another word and walked away.

I spent a few minutes making sure I looked like a goddess, then confidently walked into the pool area and headed for the spa to relax and sober up. It wasn't particularly busy, and only one man sat in the water when I climbed into the warm bubbles."Oh God, I hope my fake tan doesn't make the water turn green!" I giggled like a schoolgirl as I sat down, expecting the stranger to respond. He looked at me slightly scared and didn't say a thing.

"Chlorine and fake tan?" I quizzed him, as if he should understand. He nodded, but looked uncomfortable, then stood and got out. Since today was all about guys walking away from me and not giving a sh*t, it didn't surprise me. I tilted my head back and closed my eyes. After a few minutes' relaxation I was joined again, this time by the older woman whom I'd crossed in the changing rooms.

"Look, I'm sorry for speaking to you that way. I've had a really bad day, please don't make it any worse. I didn't mean to be rude."

"It's okay." She smiled at me softly."Would you like to talk about it?" She offered a sympathetic ear, and her unexpected kindness brought me close to tears.

"I'm not sure you would be able to empathise with me, it's very complicated." I stared into space, trying to control my emotions.

"My husband was a vicar; I've heard just about everything. You won't shock me." She seemed worldly and wise, and I felt like I could open up.

"I'm in love with an emotionally dead, unavailable older man. It's evident now that he's absolutely not in love with me." I expected her to get up and walk out in complete disgust at my admission. She took a few minutes to process the information before responding.

"A man who loves you will show he loves you in every way he can. He'll not let you down or disappoint you. He'll cherish you and never let you go. There are some very mixed-up people in this world. It's not your fault." She reached over, squeezed my shoulder, and gave me a reassuring smile.

"Our daughter's been through what you're going through, but she was on the online dating sites and he gaslighted her. It was a terrible carry on. It'll just work its way out of you eventually, when you learn how to love yourself. You won't let this happen again after that." She spoke from parental pain; I could see it in her face."Do you believe in God?" She looked at me in hope."He can help you."

"When I was younger, I did, but now I'm not sure what I believe. Life's a horrible place most of the time. It makes me question how God could create us and let us experience so much pain. Thank you for not judging me," I said sincerely, lifting myself out of the water.

"It was my pleasure. Please look after yourself and know your worth. Oh, and next time, share the champagne!" She winked, then closed her eyes. I smiled widely, nodded, and walked away.

The steam room was empty when I entered it, so I found a spot and lay down on my back with my knees up. My head spun as the alcohol hit me, and I felt like I needed to sleep, or possibly vomit. The door opened, then closed, but my eyes remained shut."Hello again," a deep, well-to-do voice spoke to me. I opened one eye but didn't move.

"Oh, hi," I said unemotionally, then closed that eye again.

"Do you come here often?" he continued. I wanted him to just shut up so I could fall asleep in the steam.

"Yes, I'm a member. You?"

"A day pass, I just thought I'd try it out. It's quite nice," he continued to bother me.

"The pool is too small and there's not enough fit men," I said dryly.

"You're single?" He sounded surprised.

"Yes, 100% single." I reflected and immediately felt deflated.

"Well, single is the new black." He tried to pacify me.

"Only people in relationships say that." I snapped.

"Not at all. But you seem in good shape, and healthy body, healthy mind. Strong women don't need men?" His words were rushed out nervously.

"I stay in shape because I have a lot of sex. You should try it!" I responded, hoping to make him uncomfortable enough to leave me in peace.

"Best offer I've had all day," he said shyly back. I sat up and looked at him. To my delight, he was handsome. "You didn't turn the water green then?" he said amused, and I shook my head slowly in acknowledgment. "So, what do you do for a living?" He seemed mesmerised by me.

"I'm a writer." I spoke without thinking.

"A published writer?" he continued to question me.

"Yes, I'm currently writing my second book," I said proudly, but my mind drifted back to Fox, and I felt uncomfortable with myself.

"I'm a journalist, I work for the BBC. What do you write? Will I know of it?" He seemed delighted and intrigued, his body leaned toward me.

"Erotic books. I'm writing a trilogy. It's a true story about my life since I left my god-awful marriage." I looked down at the floor.

"So, you write about sex?" His voice broke, and he gulped.

"I write about love, dating, and sex. It's different to all other books that've been written, as it's unique to my personal experience. I don't hold anything back; I speak the truth about everything."

"I guess I'm a case study?" he asked. I stared at his legs in the steam to avoid judgement.

"It's my fortieth birthday today." I quickly changed the subject as I could see he'd crossed his legs.

"You don't look a day over thirty." He looked at me in surprise."Why are you all alone on your birthday?"

"I've had a bit of bad luck with men. I had a day of epic shagging planned, but he didn't turn up." I sighed and laid back down, closing my eyes again.

"I'm sorry to hear that. Are you okay?" I didn't answer.

"So, Mr Journalist, how long have you worked for the BBC?" Deflecting was the only way I could get through not crying, not that he would've seen my tears because of the steam.

"Since forever. It's a great job. I have lots of contacts if you need any help or advice? What's your book called?" He suddenly became very focused.

"My first book's called A Year of Tiramisu, and I haven't settled on a title for my second. My pen name is L.J. Brown."

"What does L.J. stand for?" he continued to question me.

"L is for liberty, liberation, and freedom. It's how I felt when I left my marriage. J is for Jane, because Jane Austen is my favourite author."

"That's hilarious. What does Brown stand for? Is it your surname?" He wiped the steam from his face and pushed his hair back.

"I'm afraid that's the least smart part. I was in a coffee shop opening some brown sugar, suffering from a terrible hangover, and it just came to me. I thought it was brilliant at the time. I was probably still a little bit drunk." I laughed and he laughed with me.

"I love it." He clapped his hands together, splashing water everywhere.

"I'm going to get out of here, I need a cold shower. Do you want to join me in the sauna?" I slowly stood and started to walk toward the door so he could take a good look at my bottom.

"Lead the way." He promptly stood and followed me out. I leaned under the shower and let him wait for his turn before heading to the sauna. Sitting in one corner of the room was an overweight man who nodded and said hello. I found a seat and waited for the journalist to join me.

He opened the door and I saw him more clearly. He was tall, lean, and I could tell he worked out. He looked like he was in his late forties. His sideburns were turning grey, and his laughter lines were prominent. His eyes were beautiful, and he never took them off me.

"So, are you on social media? How do I get in contact with you?" He didn't give up on the interrogation.

"I can tell you're a journalist." I pulled at my bikini top to make my breasts more comfortable.

"I'd love to interview you. Are you on LinkedIn?" He fished for answers.

"I'm on LinkedIn, yes, but I'm not famous or anything so it wouldn't be much of a story for you. Sales are slow; my last royalties paid for a

Chinese takeaway."

"Then you need publicity." He was now animated, and I saw how passionate he was about his job.

"Well, okay, sure, let's stay connected then, I guess." I shrugged and laid back down in the heat.

"One other question; why are you struggling with the title for your next book?" He tilted his head back and relaxed.

"It just won't come to me. So far, I have A Year of Sin." I gave a large sigh of frustration."The first book came to me so quickly. Tiramisu, 'pick me up, lift me up'—it was a feel-good dessert I ate after being dumped, but this is driving me insane. I've lived a year in SIN. I'm separated but still married, so in the eyes of God, I'm a sinner. That's all I have to go on." I looked at him for inspiration.

"Okay, well, what stands out in the time that you've been seeing him?" He looked slightly worried about where all this was going.

"The sex, I guess. It's out of this world." I felt a clench in my stomach as I recalled the memories."And he sings to me, old stuff that I wouldn't usually listen to, but I love it."

"What kind of music?"

"Sinatra, Elvis, Dean Martin…"

"How old is he?"

"Fifty-four," I said under my breath.

"That's a big age gap. Do you have daddy issues?" he said jokingly. I gave him a sarcastic look.

"Age is just a number. I like older men; they're better in bed, and more interesting."

"A year of SINatra," he said out of nowhere, and I sat bolt upright.

"Yes! That's brilliant. You're a genius! I don't know how to thank you." My head filled with possibilities. I got up and rushed for the door.

"Where are you going? You didn't give me your real name." He stood up, surprised.

"I need to write while I'm inspired." I looked back at him and smiled brightly."You'll figure out who I am, you're a journalist."

I left the sauna and practically ran back to the changing room to get dressed, then rushed home to log on to my laptop. I spent the rest of my fortieth birthday deep in thought and creativity, doing what I loved to do best—writing my story.

CHAPTER TWELVE

"In My Mind" ~ Gigi D'Agostino

Being alone was something I'd grown used to, especially now that I was a writer. I spent a lot of time locked away in my own head trying to understand myself and figure out how to articulate my story for the world to read. Whenever my heart felt broken, I became even more obsessed with writing, and less in control of my thoughts and feelings. Sometimes writing felt like a curse; it was something I couldn't hide from or put down. In the back of my mind, I would always be thinking, what do I need to write next?

One evening, I sat on my bed with my laptop and stared at the pages I'd written, scrolling through endless memories from times I'd spent with Fox over the last twelve months. I tried to format it in some kind of logical order so it would make sense to my readers, but it felt like an impossible task. I poured a glass of wine and turned on my playlist to get into the zone. Tonight, something wasn't quite working the way it usually did. I couldn't get comfortable on my bed or at my desk. I was filled full of energy, wired, and uncomfortable with myself—my creativity was not flowing.

"What the F*CK is wrong with me? I never get writer's block!" I shouted at the computer screen, frustrated with myself. I swigged the glass of wine down and paced around the room, loosening my shirt and taking my belt off.

"Okay, so I have the first chapter, 'New York, New York.' Exit Mr Fancy Pants. Let's get on with the real story. F*ck, balls, sh*t! This is ALL in the wrong order!" I pushed my laptop away and put my face in my hands. I looked around my room; it had a double bed, a desk, a chest of drawers, and books everywhere.

"I need space. I need order," I said to myself. I got up off the bed, placed my laptop on the desk, and gathered the sheets up off the bed, then the mattress, and moved them to another bedroom. I came back and looked at the bed for a few minutes, contemplating what to do."Well, as there's no shagging going on tonight and I'm far from sleepy, I don't need you." I shook my finger at the bed, grinned, then lifted it and dragged it onto the landing.

I moved my desk into the middle of the room, pulled up the chair, and sat down. I picked up my glass of wine and rocked it from side to side before taking another gulp. This book was important. Forget A Year of Tiramisu; this was my signature book, the book that had to become a best seller, the sexiest thing I'd ever written, and the book that would make Fox fall in love with me once he'd read about us and our fantastic sex life.

I looked around at my empty walls and had a brilliant idea. I pulled my desk drawer open and took out some A4 sheets of paper. On each sheet I wrote a chapter number from one to twenty-six, then found some Blu-Tack and strategically stuck the sheets on my wall.

"Something's still not right." I scratched my head and looked all around until I caught a glimpse of my refection in the bedroom mirror."Of course, I've got clothes on. I always write better naked!" I looked at myself and laughed, quickly undressing, throwing my clothes around the room and jumping up and down in the space around me.

"Music!" I clapped my hands together and instructed my Alexa."Alexa, the Sinatra playlist please." She spoke back to me in her usual polite manner and started playing the collection of his work. I flicked through the chapters one by one and wrote down on the sheets of paper how I thought they should be ordered, then changed them around several times, getting more and more tipsy.

'Strangers in the Night' came on the playlist and my heart pounded as I recalled the first time I'd made love to the silver fox. I closed my eyes and danced around the room, just like I'd done in the hotel room that night, giving him a private dance before he got to touch my body. I opened my eyes, and I imagined him on the bed watching me, taking in his little 'gipsy,' as he described me, dancing around naked with a glass of wine. I pretended he was with me now.

"Fox, how am I ever going to finish this book when I don't know the ending? What do you want from me? Why don't you love me?" I closed my eyes and desperately tried to empty my mind of him when my phone rang. I couldn't believe it! This happened all the time now—I'd think of him, and he'd call or turn up at the house.

"Hello?" he said softly.

"Hello, Fox. What can I do for you?" I sat on the floor and looked at the wall with all my notes on it.

"What are you up to this evening?" he questioned me but seemed distant.

"Well, I've written book two, but don't have the ending yet, and I'm struggling to get it all in order to send to the publisher." I took another gulp of wine and let out a big sigh."What are you doing tonight?" I quickly changed the subject.

"I'm sat in a hotel room on the phone to you." His sexy voice was now calm, and my mind raced, wanting to be with him.

"L.J., are you really stuck? Do you need me to help you? I was a participant, after all," he smirked down the phone.

"Can you spare the time?" I blushed."Can we FaceTime? I've had to rearrange my room to work. I couldn't think. You need to be able to see the wall."

"Crazy girl. Yes, switch over to FaceTime." He took in a deep breath.

"Hi, you." I looked at his face his eyes widened.

"L.J., you're naked!" he snorted out a wicked laugh.

"Oh, sh*t, yes, sorry. I often write with no clothes on; it helps me feel freer to express myself." I smiled widely."Do you want me to put some clothes on?" I bit my lip and blushed again.

"No, naked's fine." His eyes scanned my body like he was starving for sex with me."God, I love looking at your tits." He was distracted.

"Fox, concentrate; I need your memory," I told him off sweetly, and he shut his eyes in frustration."Okay, so you remember A Year of Tiramisu had twenty-six chapters? I want the same for the second book. The first chapter is a filthy dream, which unfortunately is about Fancy Pants." I got up and paced around the room."I had to open with him to make readers see that he was still on my mind when we first met."

"How does it end?" he quizzed me.

"He stuck a dildo up my ass!" I laughed loudly, and my voice echoed around the room.

"And this was a dream or a fantasy, L.J.?" he teased, but didn't sound jealous. I shook my head at him.

"I don't think a dildo would fit." I pulled a pained face, then laughed."So, all the chapter names are after a Sinatra song as it's the title of the book, and you got me into him in the first place. The second chapter is, 'The Lady is a Tramp.'"

He pursed his lips."I'm saying nothing," he teased.

"It's the trip in the car to meet you for the presentation, when you pencilled me in for 'dinner.'" I used my fingers to indicate speech marks."You had it all planned, didn't you?" I searched his face for answers.

"Nope. I promise I never had any expectation of sleeping with you. It was you who suggested it as a possibility." He scratched his beard and looked into my eyes; they were filled with memories of that night—I could see him imagining it.

"So, 'Strangers in the Night' was the first sex scene of the book, when I f*cked the presentation up, got drunk, and danced around your hotel room naked with a bottle of wine." I pointed to the wall.

"Strangers in the night, exchanging glances, wandering in the night…" he began to sing the song to me.

"Stop it, we need to concentrate." I interrupted him mid-song, but I did love his voice.

"Every man in that restaurant's jaw nearly dropped to the floor when you walked in wearing those tight leather pants, you sexy bitch," he reflected.

"Confidence is sexy, not me." I started to type some notes on my laptop. I would never take a full compliment.

"I was drunk that night, but I felt really comfortable with you." I didn't look at him and continued typing.

"That was a night of sex I will never ever forget as long as I live."

"Because I nearly flooded the hotel room?" I said sarcastically.

"No, because it was our first, and it was exceptional. Normally, the first time's a bit of a disaster, from experience."

"You read my first book, you knew what to expect; I'm a bit of an expert," I said with complete confidence. Sex was something I knew I was really good at.

"The way you sucked my cock blew me away—literally! You know what you're doing!" He fell back on the bed and showed me his hard cock over the shared screen.

"Fox, put it away, and concentrate." I covered my eyes, then peeped through my fingers. He hit his phone with his penis, trying to get my attention.

"Show me your pussy; I want to be inside you again," he demanded.

"Maybe," I said, giving him a wicked glance of lust.

"Okay, okay. I'm concentrating." He sat back up on his bed and put a pillow behind his head. My eyes directed him to his erect penis."Put it away, Fox, it's distracting me!"

"He doesn't want to." He put his hands in the air and grinned.

"So, then we see each other and talk more, then start to become addicted to the sex. Chapter seven, 'Fly me to the Moon,' was when you f*cked me with a cucumber and drank Champagne out of my pussy." I looked at his raised eyebrows.

"F*cking hell, that was a proper good f*ck." He ran his fingers through his hair, then pointed at his massive penis.

"Let's skip chapter eight." I scrolled down to the next chapter.

"Why, what did we do?" I ignored him. I didn't want him to know it was the moment I realised I loved him; it would spoil the mood.

"Now, this is where my memory's not good. Did the cucumber sex come before the time I took all my clothes off in a field and my panties got stuck on a cow's head?" I asked, trying to sound innocent.

"After." He clapped his hands together and belly laughed, rolling around his bed in amusement."You gave me a mouthful of abuse in the car too." He remembered our first fight.

"Well, you deserved it." I looked at him lovingly, knowing we each played our part. I got up and switched the chapters around into chronological order.

"What did you call the chapter?"

"Call me irresponsible."

"That's very fitting." He was extremely amused by now and had changed his position to mirror mine, lying down on his front, paying attention."What's next?"

"Publishing deals, work, more Fancy Pants, radio interviews, photoshoots. I think they're all in order. Then, the hotel room for your birthday, me wearing the black stockings and suspenders and the giant red bow!"

"God, what a surprise that was!" He looked at me in awe.

"I love surprises… and you're welcome." I blew him a kiss and he caught it.

"I was amazed that you managed to throw your bangles onto my cock and not miss." We laughed hysterically, like children.

"Then the ending so far is when you came to my new house, and I wore the Sinatra hat. We literally bounced off every wall and floor in the house—it was sensational. But I'm not sure the story's finished; I can't quite get it right." I laid on my side now looking at him and the wall filled full of scribbles, my mind racing with ideas of how to make the book better.

"I loved our first year together. It was like a dream come true, even if you were a pain in the ass." I gave him a warning look and he backed off."You forgot the pub with the dog that knocked over your drink, and you sat on my face in the hotel room and covered me, then I f*cked you up the ass in the shower."

"That was one of my favourites. How could I forget it?" I'd loved that date.

"You better get writing, young lady." He looked at his watch, and it was getting late.

"Phone sex first?" I walked to the shower and turned it on, getting in.

"You sexy little temptress!" He stared at me as if his eyes would pop out of their sockets as I played.

"So, I wrote you a book, Fox." I took my hand out of my pussy and licked my fingers."What are you going to do for me in return?" I loved teasing him.

Standing so I could see his erection through the phone, he replied,"I'm going to f*ck you at every opportunity, for the rest of your life! Get to Liverpool, as soon as possible."

CHAPTER THIRTEEN

"Back to Black" ~ Amy Winehouse

"You can do this," I told myself assertively, while brushing my teeth and looking at my reflection in the mirror. My usual hangover and tiredness didn't help with the long drive to Liverpool and the conversation I'd prepared to have with Fox. After my birthday, and the realisation that the relationship with Fox was going nowhere fast, the possibility that he only wanted me for sex was constantly on my mind. I needed answers, to know what this was to him.

I'd finished the book and printed it to take with me for him to read, to convince him just how good we were together. I'd lost weight and stopped paying attention to myself. I didn't care about fake tans and perfect nails. I'd become a hermit, writing and hiding away from everyone in a world of make believe. Drinking was the only way I could deal with my emotions. I was turning into someone I didn't recognise because of this man. It felt like I was going slowly insane, because it was so real for me, but it didn't seem to be for him.

I turned on the shower, hit my playlist, and got in, slowly lathering my body in soap. It'd been a while since I'd even shaved my legs—this wasn't like me. I made an effort to have a perfectly smooth body and beautifully washed hair, so that when I faced him today, I didn't look unkempt. Steam filled the washroom because I'd been in far too long, slowly dancing around, trying to feel my heart beat to the rhythm of the music, hoping it could feel alive again.

Like a zombie, I stepped out and wrapped myself in a towel. I closed my eyes. I'd wrapped myself in this towel with him. I was clinging onto every memory of him, and it was driving me to madness. Standing in front of the mirror, I brushed my long dark hair, untangling its wild ways. Wiping the steam off the mirror, I applied my foundation, paying attention to the dark circles underneath my eyes and adding more concealer than usual to disguise them. Black eyeliner was next; it followed the shape of my big blue eyes, making them look even bigger. After painting my eyelashes to make them lush with volume, I moved onto defining my out-of-control eyebrows, which needed attention. Finally, I reached for my red lipstick and began to paint it on my bottom lip, pursing them together and blotting with a piece of tissue. I knew how much he loved red lipstick and remembered it being smudged all over his face every time we kissed.

This would be the last time I was going to see him if I didn't get the answer I wanted, so I'd thought hard about what I would wear. I decided that the same clothes I wore the first night we were together would be a perfect parting reminder of how good we were together. I couldn't wear any panties with the skinny leather trousers, or they would show through the material, which was so tight to my skin. Pulling them up my legs, I closed my eyes and remembered him looking at me while I was sliding them down and kicking them to one side. The eye contact we'd had still burned through my soul. Next was no bra and an off the shoulder black top that you could see the shape of my breasts and my nipples through.

I bent over, tossing my hair around, running my fingers through it, creating volume, and spraying it with perfume. I continued to dance to my playlist, squirting Euphoria behind my ears, on my neck, and wrists. Something was missing from this devilish look as I stared at my reflection in hope that I'd replicated a former me—one he would want again.

"Heels," I told myself in the mirror. Slowly, I slipped on black stilettoes, which made me taller than the mirror so I couldn't see my face anymore, only my long legs. I slowly turned around in a circle and observed my body before tilting the mirror back to look at my face once more. Taking a deep sigh, I grabbed my bag, red lipstick, and his favourite light blue denim jacket.

"Alexa, stop. I have a date with a devil," I said with attitude in my voice. Gathering my car keys, I headed for the door, then stopped and leaned my head against it.

"What if he says no?" I asked pathetically. Composing myself, I took the paper with the address of where we were supposed to meet, my hand shaking from emotion, my heart thumping loudly. Opening the door, I clicked my car unlocked and walked slowly to it in my heels with my head down.

I tapped the postcode into the satnav, and it told me the estimated time to my destination. I took a screenshot and sent it to Fox. Within minutes I had a reply."I'll see you soon. I expect you to get lost. Just call me for directions," his reply felt cold, patronising, and empty, like his heart had become. I released the handbrake reluctantly, turned the heating on to try and stop myself shaking, then set off.

It took twenty minutes longer than I'd anticipated. I asked for directions twice from locals. I refused to let him know I'd got lost or contact him for advice. The area I was entering was awful, possibly the roughest place I'd ever seen. Streets of back-to-back houses with rubbish piled high everywhere, and people hanging around on street corners looking like they were up to no good. It was scary, dark, and depressing. As I searched for somewhere to park in a narrow street, I called him.

"Hello, Fox. I think I'm here, but I'm not sure if the satnav has sent me to the wrong place?" I said nervously, looking around me and feeling unsafe. People stared at me in my car from twitching curtains or stood smoking outside their front doors.

"Yes, look to your right." I shifted my glance quickly to the right of me and he stood at a doorway waving with one hand, his phone in the other. I looked at him startled and nodded in acknowledgment. My heart sank. I felt sick, scared, and thought about turning around and just going back home.

"I'll be right with you," I replied, my voice shaking. I looked around and closed my eyes, taking a deep breath, getting myself prepared for what I'd rehearsed to say to him and how I was going to control the situation. I stopped the engine, looked in the mirror to re-apply my red lipstick, put the manuscript in my bag, cricked my stiff neck from driving, got into character and stepped out of the car. A stranger gave me a wolf whistle in the street. I stopped and looked at him with a glance of disgust.

"Fox," I said assertively, as he gestured for me to walk inside, closing the door behind me.

"I want my house key back." I held out my hand in anticipation. We'd agreed over text earlier in the week that he would hand it back.

"Why have you come dressed like this?" He hovered over me, my back now pressed to the door, so I couldn't make an escape.

"I dressed like this the first time we met," I confidently spat out my words.

"So I'd want to f*ck you?" He stared at me intensely, his eyes redirecting mine to the bulge in his pants.

"So we could talk. I just came to, well, I wanted to say that…" I stood tall, backed up against the door."What a sh*t hole!" I continued, as my eyes left him and looked around the room I was standing in. The house made me feel uneasy and unwelcome.

"I bought it to help someone out, but never viewed it; it was an investment." He looked me up and down, then backed away.

"What do you want, L.J.? You've driven all this way to talk to me, to get your key back? Really?" He looked at me as if it were a joke.

"I can't continue this relationship with you unless you commit to me." I looked right into his eyes, trying not to break my confidence.

"I'm sorry," he said gently into my ear, stroking my hair away from my face and kissing my cheek. Our eyes were locked.

"My key please." I held out my hand.

"You're not going anywhere," he said, pinning his body against mine. His hard cock pressed against me through his trousers.

"My key!" I persisted, my breath starting to shorten as his mouth kissed mine, and we were like animals.

"Here's your f*cking precious key," he said, putting it down his pants.

"We're not doing this Fox." I tried to resist him, but my body wanted him just as much as he wanted mine.

"Oh yes, we are, L.J. I'm going to f*ck you against this door," he said in a seductive low voice. I kissed him with my red lipstick all over his face. I wondered what I looked like to him.

He pushed my top up over my shoulders and grabbed my breast, biting and sucking me like he never had before. Forcing his weight onto me, he kept me pinned to the door so I couldn't escape.

He pulled down my leather pants and dropped to his knees, fingering me furiously and sticking his tongue deep inside me. His other hand made sure I stayed where I was. I couldn't speak, I couldn't think, and I couldn't stop what was happening. My legs were about to give in to the pleasure and I started to slide down the door.

He undressed me, bit by bit, kissing me hard, not taking his eyes off me, then picked me up and took me to another room."You're so wet… We're going to have some fun," he said in his deep sexy Liverpool accent.

"I don't like it here, Fox, I feel uncomfortable," I said nervously, kissing him back and brushing his face with my hand.

"Why? Don't be silly," he said reassuringly.

"This house has eyes." I looked at him scared and he looked amused.

"No one else is here," he smirked and scratched his head.

"I don't know, Fox; I feel weird. Something's not right." I searched his eyes for an answer. I felt the air turn cold and heard a faint whisper in my ear telling me to 'GET OUT'. I reached for his hand and squeezed it tightly for protection.

"It's been rumoured to be haunted." He laughed and put me down."We think we might have evidence." He reached for his phone."Look at this photo taken in the front room when I put it up for sale." He showed me a photo of a distorted shadow of a face wearing a top hat only a few steps away from where we'd been standing. My blood felt cold.

"I really don't like this house, Fox," I said pulling him toward me tightly.

"Are you psychic, L.J.? That's really quite something, even gave me goosebumps when I saw it. Come on, I'll show you around the house so you can see no one is here but us."

"No, I don't want to," I protested.

"Okay, will you calm down please?" He looked at me, worried.

"Fox, we need to talk." He let go of his grip and I backed away from him a few steps.

"I know you do; I've felt like this has been coming for weeks." He walked toward the kitchen and leaned against one of the units with his arms folded."Can I go first?" He lowered his voice and looked away from me.

"I guess," I said, feeling my heart pound with anxiety, hoping he wouldn't break up with me. I jumped up onto the sink naked and sat there paying him my full attention.

He walked toward me and grabbed my hand gently, moving it toward his neck and placing my hand around it, then he took my other hand and placed it at the other side of his neck."Feel," he said gently, looking into my eyes sadly, waiting for my reaction. I tentatively took my time feeling both sides and felt a lump on the left side. Pulling my hand away, I took a sharp breath and looked at him in shock, tears welling in my eyes.

"I've been feeling unwell for a while," he said slowly and softly,"since just before your birthday."

"How unwell?" I started to sob, my head spinning with shock.

"L.J., I have throat cancer." He looked at me, scared, but holding it together.

"I'm sorry, you have WHAT? It's 100 percent confirmed?" I choked my words out, not able to see him for tears, suddenly feeling the shame of being naked.

"I start chemotherapy in a few weeks. I'm going to fight the f*ck out of it, and the recovery rates are quite high." He tried to reassure me, squeezing my hand tightly."We won't be able to see each other for some time, and I won't always be able to respond to messages when I'm in treatment," he continued, as if he'd thought of everything before having the conversation with me.

"Is that why you didn't come to see me on my birthday?" I questioned him and felt instantly guilty.

"L.J., I'd have been there if I could. I hope you understand." I felt like I was going to be sick. I've cursed him and been mad at him, and it wasn't even his fault that he couldn't make my birthday.

"I'll stand by you." I jumped to my feet and moved into him, holding him like I never wanted to let go."I'll support you." I looked at him as he wiped away the tears from my face. His body tensed and I could tell he felt uncomfortable by my show of emotions."You can keep the key. You can stay at my house. You can do anything. I will do anything for you," I pleaded."I love you, Fox, please don't die. I can't survive without you. You're my air."

"I'll come back to you when I'm better." He lifted my chin, tears dripping off it.

"I don't want you to, to..."

"Die?" He finished my sentence, and I nodded."We all have to die one day. If it's my time, then it's just the way things have to be," he said, like it wasn't really that big a deal."But you were going to finish it anyway today, were you not?" He looked away now.

"No, I wasn't. I was going to try to get you to stay with me forever," I sniffed. It now felt completely selfish.

"Never going to happen, especially now," he said unemotionally.

"But what about the past twelve months?" I stood in the kitchen, my naked body filled with emotional charge.

"Fun, L.J., blissful fun. I've adored your company." He crossed his arms defensively and started to fidget.

"Sex, that's it? Nothing more? Not friendship? Not love?" I couldn't understand.""But I just told you how I feel. You've seen my emotions; this is real for me." I felt deflated and frustrated—nothing made sense.""Why are you pushing me away, Fox? Because you're sick? You think I'll get scared? I won't. I can handle this."

"I told you before, I don't feel love; I've always been honest about that." I fell to the floor and sobbed; he bent down to meet me and awkwardly tried to comfort me."Pull yourself together. You'll move on with or without me. Get up." He pulled me up off the cold floor and I tried to stop crying, taking shallow breaths.

"I better get my clothes and leave." I glanced at him bewildered and walked toward the living room where I felt a shiver again.

"I don't just pick up anyone, you know," he shouted after me, trying to contain the situation.

I gathered my things."You've clearly picked not to be with me." I gulped and again felt like I was going to be sick.

"We can't leave each other like this, and you can't drive home in this state." He grabbed my arm and pulled me toward him. I felt his heart beating. What he was saying and feeling didn't match up; I was so confused.

"I'm fine. I understand. I want you to do all the things that make you happy, and whatever you need to do to get you through this." I bit my lip to stop it quivering and he kissed it.

"L.J., please, this seriously might be the last time we see each other." He ran his fingers through my hair."Let's make love one last time?" He squeezed his hardon into me, and I pressed my head against his chest, inhaling his scent deeply, feeling reassured by the familiar smell of Hugo Boss. "Kiss me like you're going to miss me," he quoted the Deadpool movie line, and I grinned through my tears. He was trying to make light of the situation, even though it felt like the world had just ended for me.

"I'll miss you so much," I said, devastated, kissing him furiously. The heat of his body touched mine as he lifted off his top. He never said it back.

"Get back up on the sink," he ordered me, and I did as instructed. He pulled my legs to the edge and dropped his pants to the floor. "I'm going to open the blind so people can watch us." He reached for the cord.

"What? Wait! No," I protested, but it was too late. He was inside me with one thrust. I saw people walking up and down the street as my head banged on the window with the motion. He kissed me so hard all over my body, biting and sucking me until I was sore. He really wanted to have this last time, perhaps because he thought he might never have another one.

"Someone will report us," I screamed, close to climax, worried, but surprisingly turned on at the same time. He picked me up off the sink.

"Don't make a sound," he ordered, as he picked up pace and pounded me harder and harder. I wanted to scream but couldn't. Looking at him helplessly while I climaxed, I peaked, and the force of it pushed his cock out of me. He exploded at the same time, covering me and the floor in cum. He kissed me, then stood back looking triumphant. "Look at the mess we just created. Jesus."

"Come on, let's get you dressed. You're right, it's freezing." He walked inside, pulled his pants up, and put his arms around me protectively. He gathered my trail of clothes from the floor and handed them to me."I believe these are yours. Either that or the ghost's," he jested. I smirked, still recovering from the shock, and the sex, and took them from him.

"Where's the bathroom? I need to clean up."

"The ground floor one is just behind you. I'll grab us a coffee and be back in ten minutes." He put his top back on and reached for his car keys.

"No, don't leave me in this house. I'm fine. I'll be a few minutes, then we can leave," I said anxiously. He sighed deeply and threw his car keys onto the counter. I cleaned up as fast as I could and dressed quickly, checking my face in a cracked mirror in the bathroom for smeared lipstick before re-joining him."Okay, I'm ready to go home." I brushed past him heading toward the door.

"Wait, L.J., I did remember what you were wearing the first night we met, and you did look stunning today—still do."

"I'll never forget our first time, Fox. It was special, wasn't it?" I was desperate for him to connect with me, say something, anything to suggest he loved me, that there was hope.

"Come on, I'll walk you out." He dropped his head and didn't look at me again, continuing to walk right past me. He grabbed the mail off the side and waited for me to walk out before him, then locked the door behind us.

"Do you want me to guide you out of Liverpool? You can follow me?" he suggested, looking at my fragile state.

"No, it's okay, I'm fine." I smiled, unconvincingly. Heading toward my car, a penny caught my eye in the middle of the road. I stopped and picked it up, then walked back toward him, placing the penny in his hand."For luck, Fox." I looked at him, tears filled my eyes again, but I managed to smile at him widely. I reached inside my bag, pulled out the manuscript and gave it to him."It's finished. I wanted you to be the first to have a copy of our book." I kissed his forehead."Goodbye, Fox." I held his hand.

"Goodbye, L.J.," he replied, slowly letting go of my grasp. We turned away and got into our cars. We both looked at each other one last time, and I watched him drive away, then stop. I thought he was going to change his mind and turn around, but instead he got out of his car carrying the manuscript and threw it into a nearby bin.

Back to the New York Times reporter.

"Wow, Cancer, that's just awful, it must have been quite a shock for both of you, so you were just left in limbo", and he also didn't care about the book?" Adam looked at me in disbelief and shock,"you poor thing"he reached out and squeezed my hand for support.

"I can't imagine how he was feeling, knowing that he faced dying, and that perhaps it was the last time he would see me, maybe he couldn't face reading about us","I felt so lost and sad, and that life was cruel, I think this made me fall even more deeply in love with him, but he just pushed me away". A tear rolled down my face and Adam offered me a box of tissue from the office table.

"I was so deeply in love" I whimpered"I was so devastated".

"I know you were, I can feel it", he shook his head in disbelief at how hard the feelings had been to cope with, and how the story was unfolding, not as he had expected.

"So, what happened next", he was on the edge of his seat in anticipation.

"Well, a few days later I had to go on the radio, BBC radio Leeds", to talk about my 2nd book, our first year together, A year of Sinatra being released by my publisher, ironically it was on Valentine's Day. I was in so much emotional pain to this day I don't know how I got through the interview, advertising a book about the man I loved, that was dying.

CHAPTER FOURTEEN
14TH FEBRUARY 2020—BBC RADIO LEEDS,
WEST YORKSHIRE

"My Funny Valentine" ~ Frank Sinatra

"L.J., Love, the alarm's gone off. Get up or you'll be late for the radio interview," my mother hollered, and I turned to look at my phone and check the time. I yawned, stretched, and dragged myself out of my slumber.

It was Valentine's Day, one of the most romantic days of the year, and I was of course single again. I'd received a few messages from my friends wishing me good luck and a happy Valentine's Day, then a photo of an ass from a guy I'd once gone on a date with. Nothing from Fox, which made me feel deeply sad, but not surprised.

I walked into my mother's kitchen and breakfast was waiting, along with a coffee to wake me up."Thanks, Mum, this is great," I said, lovingly tucking into the food. Her house was spotless, nothing ever out of place. Compared to my house, it was a palace, no kids' toys everywhere or piles of washing. I preferred my unorganised mess—it made me feel more comfortable.

"Are you nervous?" She turned to me with her glasses halfway down her nose, pouring her second cup of coffee.

"Nope," I lied, acting confident. I knew my mother, and anything I would say to let her know I was nervous would be magnified if I expressed it.

"Well, you better get showered and dressed. Look at the time." I looked at the kitchen clock. I had to leave in less than an hour if I was to make it on time.

"Sh*t." I gulped my toast down, drank the last of my coffee, and headed to the bathroom.

I hadn't thought about what I was going to say when I met with the radio producer for the second time. I knew that she'd remember me, but I was so nervous and overeager last time I'd met her that I'd made a pact with myself to not think about it until the day. What was I going to say? That the first book was sh*t and sold hardly any copies, and that the second one was hopefully going to do better? Or employ the 'fake it till I make' it attitude again and just go with the flow?

I stood in the shower and felt my nerves kick in. I began to panic about making a fool of myself. Having dried, I dressed in a tight black jumper dress, some killer heels, and my light blue denim jacket. I looked smart-casual and would pass for an artist. After a million kisses and good lucks from my mother, I was out of the house, in the car, and on my way.

Arriving at the BBC felt familiar; nothing had changed. I checked in, said who I was seeing, and sat in the waiting area where I could see the radio producer live on the screen with another guest. I fidgeted and couldn't relax. I felt like I needed a drink to calm my nerves.

"Is there a bathroom I could use?" I asked the receptionist, and she guided me to it. I locked myself in a cubical knowing I had 30 minutes to wait, reached into my bag, and got a small bottle of wine out that I'd brought in case of this very emergency. I drank it slowly and started to become calmer.

"I have to get bloody pissed to do an interview—classy! What's happened to me?" I started to feel my pulse slow down, and I took a few deep breaths, then finished the wine before returning to my seat.

"L.J. Brown?" A well-spoken voice caught my attention, and I stood up.

"Yes, that's me." I still couldn't get used to people calling me by my pen name. A well-dressed man with dark hair and glasses shook my hand.

"It's a pleasure to meet you. I've been reading about you and heard all about you from one of our journalists." He beamed at me and looked at my heels.

"You have?" I continued to shake his hand and smile at him. He had such a studious yet friendly face and made me feel perfectly at ease.

"Yes, you met him in a steam room apparently. He's here today." My mind raced as I tried to place him. Oh, the guy from the gym, the one who'd helped me come up with the book title.

"Oh my God, that's mental!" I exclaimed, then looked at the stairs and realised why he'd paid attention to my heels.

"Your work is unique. It's interesting. I read your first book and related it to my dating experience in some parts. I think you've hit a niche," he complimented me."So, you know the drill, you go in a few minutes before. When you're told to, sit down, and you're live," he went into professional mode.

"Yes, I know the drill—thanks." I looked around the studio and saw the producer through the glass talking on air; she recognised me and waved. I waved back in excitement, looking around to see if I could spot the guy from the gym, but he was nowhere in sight. How strange was it that I got the interview so fast? I bet it was to do with him, I thought, and smiled.

"Right, are you ready?" he said, nodding to the producer through the glass after a song had just started to play.

"Sure am," I said with a giddy smile and walked into the room.

"L.J., it's nice to see you again." She stood and gave me a big reassuring hug."It's great to see you too, you look great." I noticed how amazing she looked and how happy she was.

"Are you okay, any nerves?" She checked in with me before we started.

"I've just had a quick bottle of wine to stop them," I said truthfully.

"It's ten in the morning," she said startled, then laughed.

"It was a miniature bottle. It's just taken the edge off." I didn't feel judged; she seemed to pass it off like it was a normal occurrence with the job.

"Right, are you ready?" She started counting down, and I sat comfortably in my seat with the microphone next to my lips.

"Joining me now is the Yorkshire author, L.J. Brown. We first met around 18 months ago, when she wrote her first book, A Year of Tiramisu. The book charted her journey into the dating world after her marriage ended. Anyway, she's back with a new book, not yet released.

I remember you saying that you were writing the next book, and I did say to you when you were here last time to come back and see us, and here you are. And it's called A Year of Sinatra, which apparently, I get a mention in?"

"You do. You have a whole chapter."

"What?"

"Yes, a whole chapter."

"How have I ended up with a whole chapter in a book?" We both laughed."Is this because it's based on you? So, I'm thinking there's a radio interview in there?"

"Yes, that's right."

"Oh, thank God, that's a relief. So, what's the premise of the book, A Year of Sinatra, Frank Sinatra?"

"The guy I ended up seeing after Fancy Pants used to sing Sinatra to me pretty much every day." I longed for him to do it again and started to well up with tears.

"Which song?"

"Every song under the sun."

"So, has all of Frank Sinatra's back catalogue got a mention in the book?"

"Yeah, pretty much," I giggled. The conversation was flowing really well."He just burst into song all the time, whenever he spoke to me on the phone. If I was having a down day, he kept singing to me."

"When I was 21," she started to sing, and I laughed. She was so engaged in the conversation, and we were having fun.

"I know, totally, and he was a fantastic singer."

"Gosh."

"I used to tell him, 'Just get on with it, sing to me, carry on.'" I did my girly laugh.

"So, what's the story? Does it pick up from A Year of Tiramisu?"

"Yeah. A Year of Tiramisu kind of ended on a big cliff hanger and all the readers were like, 'Oh my God, what's going to happen next?' So, I had to continue with the second book. I'd started drafting it when I was here last, but I wasn't fully prepared for what I was going to write. It's amazing, though. I'm really proud of this book."

"Some things just take time, don't they?"

"They do. They just evolve, and you need to do more things in your life, so you have more experience."

"And every chapter is named after a Sinatra song?"

"A Frank Sinatra song, yes," I replied proudly, loving his music.

'So, what's the first chapter called?"

"Erm, New York, New York." I giggled.

"So, does it start in New York?"

"It's a dream and it's…"

"Does it end with My Way?" She laughed loudly.

"No, it doesn't. It ends with, I Can't Believe I'm Losing You."

"Aww, that's a gorgeous song as well."

"It is. It's beautiful, but when I was researching and I read about him and the Rat Pack, I was amazed by the stories."

"Oh, it's fascinating, the whole Rat Pack story and everything, and the rivalry between them."

"They were little monkeys."

"They were little monkeys, weren't they? Just to be there in the middle of it all with Dean Martin and Sammy Davis, Jr., just all of that era."

"Listening to them is amazing, the depth of the music and what they were going through. Some of them were quite lost, I think, and they found themselves in music." I reflected on this and thought how lost I'd been and how much their music had helped me.

"They drowned themselves in drink and sorrow, so the music was coming from some kind of deep pain. I don't know, but the more I read and researched it, the more it became involved in my book. So, it's actually very psychologically cool."

I didn't say that how I wanted to, but it will have to do, I thought to myself.

"So, this all stems—I love this—from a guy you were seeing, but aren't seeing any more?"

"No, not at all. Me and Mr Fancy Pants are a thing of the past."

"Does he know about this book?"

"He's listening right now."

"He's listening?" She gasped."So, you've told him he's a thing of the past, and he's listening. So, you've got a good friendship?"

"Nope, we hate each other." I snorted and laughed.

"You must still speak?"

"We spoke until a few months ago. Four years ago, I met him on online dating."

"But how does he know that this is on now?"

"He follows me on Snap, with stuff that I post about the books."

"Right, okay. You know you're destined to be together and get married, don't you?"

"What, me and Fancy Pants? Do you really think so?" I know I sounded like a giddy child.

"Yeah, it's going to happen. It's one of those relationships that goes round in circles."

"No, it's a love/hate thing."

"You're going to end up married. It's going to happen. I will D.J. at your wedding."

"Will you actually?"

"Let's shake on it."

"Come on, Fancy Pants, she just shook." I laughed loudly."I've just shook. I've just shook," she repeated, laughing into the microphone."I'll do it for free," she exclaimed.

"Not interested." I looked at her in amusement.

"Anyway, more about this book. Could there be a third book?"

"Yes, I've started writing it. I have drafted an idea but want to keep listeners hungry for more."

"Gosh." She seemed amazed.

"So yeah, you know what? I didn't even know that I could write, and the first book was kind of word vomit, like, a therapeutic thing. I was going through a hard time after my divorce, and I was trying to find my confidence again. Leaving my husband after ten years was a big deal; then I got thrown into the dating scene, and I was just trying to find myself again. That's how I ended up stumbling into Fancy Pants. In the second book, I write about how when I got dumped for someone 20 years younger than me, the Fox literally just took charge, as a friend, and for three months he listened to me cry, and drink, and whine about Fancy Pants. He was there for me, unconditionally, and I'd never even met him." I reflected on that awful time and looked at the floor to stop myself crying.

"Gosh," she said softly.

"And then we saw each other for the first time, at a presentation for his company, and we just clicked, and that was it. So, for a long time, I saw him."

"So, is all this woven into the book?"

"Yes. I was at the point in my life where I didn't want to put up with anyone treating me badly. I'd just tell them to go away."

"That's great advice for anyone, because you can really get sucked into toxic relationships."

"Absolutely. Narcissistic men, I'm a magnet to them." I rolled my eyes."So yeah, he looked out for me, looked after me, and I didn't want to fall in love."

"But you did?"

"One hundred percent—the one." I blushed and wished he was listening.

"All this is in the book, isn't it?"

"Oh yes, it's a beautiful book. The first book, I would tear apart now because it's not a true representation of who I am as a person—it was a state of mind at the time. I had to write to get it all out."

"Well, they always say, don't they, whatever you're going through in life, if you're going through a hard time, don't keep it all inside, get it down on paper. I went through a really bad breakup once and wrote 25,500 words about it." She empathised with me.

"WOW!" I said, animated, throwing my hands in the air."This book is 90,000 words of 'OMG,'" I said dramatically.

"I'm going to give you some echo for that." And she did."So, if people want to buy your book, where do they get it?"

"It's out early spring; it's going to be in Waterstones, on Amazon, and at Barnes and Noble. It's everywhere that it was before. I'm back with my publisher, Pegasus. They've stuck with me through thick and thin, and rolled their eyes a few times."

My poor publisher, I thought, putting up with me; I'm no picnic.

"I think they do that with all talent, with all talent it's a rollercoaster. We're a funny breed," she said, as though understanding my pain."L.J. Brown, she's from Yorkshire, and we're proud of her."

"Yeah, Yorkshire Rose."

I don't know why I said that, I thought.

"A Year of Sinatra is out in the spring. Thank you so much for joining us."

"Thank you, BBC Radio Leeds." And it was over.

CHAPTER FIFTEEN

"Trapped" ~ Bruce Springsteen

Almost a month had passed by, and I had not heard from fox, he had made it impossible for me to reach him, and I presumed the worst. My drinking had got out of control, and I couldn't write, I'd given up on myself I didn't even care what I looked like anymore, my heart had broken, and my life felt like it was over. It was now March 2020. I'd been watching the news as things spiralled out of control quickly. Now, work had sent me home and the schools were shut. No one seemed to know what was going on, and everyone was in a state of confusion and panic and being stupid. I thought the whole world had become completely irrational and angry and insane!

Huddled together on the sofa with the children, I sat fixed to the TV screen, waiting with the rest of the nation to hear the UK prime minister's speech. It felt similar to the time the twin towers were hit; I knew I was never going to forget this moment, and my children wouldn't forget it either. History was happening in front of our eyes.

The BBC announced,"There now follows a ministerial broadcast from the prime minister," and we were silent, watching him behind a desk wearing a smart blue shirt with a horrendous red tie. I instantly thought of Fox and his hopelessly bad choice of clothes; he was even worse than Fancy Pants at complementing his eyes and complexion.

"Good evening. The Coronavirus is the biggest threat this country has faced for decades, and this country is not alone. All over the world we're seeing the devastating impact of this invisible killer." He was boldly informative and calm, but somehow strangely erratic, like a few people I'd seen in the past when they were tripping.

"Mummy, what's wrong with the prime minister's hair?" my little boy observed, clearly not listening to the words, becoming quickly bored and starting to fidget.

"It's just a bit wild; he's probably not been able to get a haircut with all the chaos. Don't be mean, Darling," I said softly, kissing him on the head."Remember what I said. Everyone is completely different and unique, and we should never judge anyone on their looks."

"I don't like his eyes either," he continued, tilting his head to one side, then sprawling halfway down the sofa and turning to look at the TV screen upside down.

"He looks weird," he continued, and I shook my head, giving up.

"I'm sure he's perfectly nice and kind." I tickled him and he sat back up the right way to cuddle me, red faced from the blood that'd rushed to his head.

"I'm going to give you one clear instruction," the prime minister continued."The time has now come for us all to do more. From this evening, I must give the British people a very simple instruction: You must stay at home!"

"WHAT? That's just NOT fair!" My daughter sprung to her feet and stormed out of the room like a typical stroppy teenager.

"We have to stay at home, Mummy? All the time?" My son frowned.

"I'm just listening to find out, Sweetheart." My forehead creased trying to listen to the rules, gradually realising that this was a bad situation.

"The way ahead is hard, and many lives will sadly be lost," he continued. I welled up and bit my lip, my mind flashing to my friends and family—and Fox.

"We'll rise to the challenge, and we'll come through it stronger than ever. We'll beat the coronavirus, and we'll beat it together. At this moment of national emergency, I ask you to stay at home, protect our NHS, and save lives. Thank you."

"Protect the NHS and save lives," my little boy mimicked the prime minster, pulling a funny face at the TV screen and blowing a raspberry."Are you okay, Mummy?" He was now lying on the floor playing with a toy car like nothing had ever happened."Does that mean no school?" He smiled at me in hope.

"I guess so." I shrugged and got down on the floor with him, my elbows on the floor and hands propping my face up, taking one of his toy cars and racing it with his.

"Yay, Mummy won't be working all the time." His words shocked me as I realised how little time I'd had to spend with him as a busy single mum. Now I wouldn't have to work and be away from him."Yay, thank you, Coronavirus!" He jumped up and danced around the room in delight. I watched with tears in my eyes over the tragedy of the world and the fact that my little boy missed his mummy.

"I'm going to check on your sister, okay? Don't go outside. Remember, our garden only for a while." He nodded and continued to play with his cars while I went upstairs.

"Can I come in?" I knocked on my daughter's door and peeked in. She was lying on her bed, playing with her phone, and didn't answer me.

"It's going to be okay you know. Just think of the positive things: time together, no school for a bit, and lots of Xbox, right?" I tried to act cool.

"But what about my friends, Mum? I'm going to miss my friends so much." She sighed as I sat next to her and offered support. My phone rang in my back pocket, and I ignored it.

"Answer it, Mum, I'm fine. Can you close my door please?" she snapped, and I knew she needed personal space to process it. I gave her a kiss and reached for my phone. I'd had a missed call from Fox. My heart sank, and I felt dizzy. It'd been so long since I'd heard anything from him. I hesitated, then pressed redial, and called him back.

"Hello?" he answered, his voice quiet and weak.

"Oh my god your alive? I was chocked up and so glad to hear from him.

"How are you L. J", his voice was weak."Well, apart from living through the f*cking apocalypse, ok I guess." I walked out into the garden and hunted for my secret, emergency stash of cigarettes.

"I had the operation and had a round of chemo," he continued, very factual, and obviously finding it difficult to talk.

"That's great. Well, it's not great… you know what I mean." I didn't know what I was talking about or how to express it.

"I just wanted to check you and the kids were okay with the news today." He genuinely seemed concerned.

"We're shocked, but fine; we just have to deal with it like everyone else, I guess." I pretended not to be scared about what was happening, but I was inwardly terrified.

"I'm going through a lot with post treatment, and I want you to know you won't be able to reach me very often, I'm sorry I blocked you, but I have never been so sick, I needed space. I'm not really talking to anyone, but it doesn't mean I'm not thinking about you, okay?" His show of affection surprised me, and I felt like there was some light in this awful situation.

"I'm thinking about you too—all the time—every day, I have fallen apart since we saw each other I love you and miss you so much." I lit a cigarette, and tears started to pour down my face, thinking of how sick he was and how much I missed him calling me daily, singing to me, and cracking awful jokes.

"keep being brave! I love you," I said, my voice breaking under the emotion.

"You can't love me, L.J. I'm a sick old man." I felt the rejection burn deep in my heart. Why would he not realise that we were supposed to be together? I knew on some level he must love me. He had to, or why would he call or reach out?

"I'm sending you a photo of the operation, so you know what I've been through. Don't share it and delete it afterward." My phone buzzed as a WhatsApp message came through to my phone. I opened it and dropped to my knees in shock. The photo showed a scar from his ear right down to the bottom of his neck with staples all the way down. They had literally cut his throat open to take away the cancer.

"Jesus Christ Almighty, are you still in pain?" I said in desperation to know he was okay.

"They've done a very good job, and I've managed with paracetamol," he said, with no emotion. He sounded flat and withdrawn; he must've been exhausted.

"Paracetamol? For f*ck's sake, why not morphine patches to keep you comfortable?"

"For God's sake, L.J., you know I don't do drugs. Calm down and stop being so emotional. I'm home, it's out, and I'm getting treatment. I consider myself lucky," he snapped and made me feel like a small child.

"Well, I'm sorry for caring so much about the man I f*cking love," I snapped back and put my cigarette out, pacing up and down the garden.

"Stop being such a drama queen," he sighed and seemed to lose interest in the conversation.

"Yes, I'm being dramatic right now, I haven't heard form you for a year, I thought you were dead, and now Bonkers Boris and his f*cked-up hair have just addressed the nation saying that we can't leave the house because a killer virus is spreading its way around the world. I think I have every right to lose the plot right now."

"Have you been drinking?" he said, clearing his throat.

"No, but I definitely need one now!"

"Typical. You'll never change," he scorned.

"You're not my dad, even if you're old enough to be," I said bitterly, and I knew it'd hit a nerve.

"It's always nice to fight, I mean… talk with you," he said sarcastically.

"What did you even call me for, Fox? You made it clear you don't want a relationship. Why are we still doing this cat and mouse chase?" I poured a glass of wine and took a large swig, noticing the mascara marks down my face in my refection on the microwave.

"You're the only person who talks to me this way. I nearly died, I'm sick, and you're yelling at me." He went silent, and this always meant he was cross.

"Just because you're sick doesn't give you the right to be a jerk! You purposely wind me up to get a reaction."

"I don't do that. This is your reaction because of your experience and personality. I'm going now. I'm not listening to this. I'm too tired—too sick." I knew any minute he was going to hang up.

"No, please, look… I'm sorry, don't go," I begged pathetically."It's just a silly fight. You know I love you," I continued.

"Goodbye, Trouble," he said softly, then hung up.

"FOX… FOX… DON'T GO!" I screamed down the phone, but it was too late."F*CK, F*CK, F*CK!" I said under my breath, trying to work out in my head what'd just happened and how I could've avoided him hanging up. My heart felt like it was going to stop. I was all consumed by him. What did any of that mean? He's clearly thinking about me.

I'd never felt so alone in my life. I walked back out into my garden with a glass of wine to get air just as the rain started to fall. I didn't feel the wetness or pitter-patter of it on my skin; I felt numb. All I could hear around me were ambulances, busy in the chaos unravelling around me. It was like being in some kind of crazy movie in slow motion—with no possible happy ending.

CHAPTER SIXTEEN

"Stayin' Alive" ~ Bee Gees

The prime minister's speeches shook the nation to its core. Boris was bonkers; it was like watching a Spitting Image puppet address the nation. I found it hard to take him seriously, especially after a glass of wine. The news was dominated by Covid-19 with every day becoming worse; numbers of cases were rising and the number of deaths across the globe were horrific. It was hard to even comprehend. I was in some kind of weird limbo, like I was watching a movie in slow motion every time I turned on the news.

I felt selfish for thinking that being locked up felt so unnatural to me, not being able to go out in my car and go to work or take the children to school. My routine of running around like a headless chicken that I'd previously complained about so much was now something I would give anything to have back. I felt like a caged animal in captivity.

I got up at the same time every day and logged on to work to check my emails, but I was only working a few hours a day and had to fill the rest of my time with other things. Work was slow and boring, and I just couldn't organise myself well working from home. I needed an office, I needed structure, and most of all I needed adult conversation. My most worrying fear was having to spend so much time with my own thoughts—it was sending me crazy.

I didn't know how long any of this would go on for, or if the human race was about to die out. I checked my phone and saw a voicemail from a Leeds number. This must be the BBC, I thought and smiled, dialled my voicemail, and listened.

"L.J., it was a pleasure to have met you at the radio interview. I've sent you a copy of the interview to your email so you can use it on social media to promote your books. I hope you are staying safe in these difficult times, Mr BBC." I hung up the phone and checked my emails; sure enough, my radio interview had been sent, along with a short message.

"I hope you don't mind, L.J., but you met one of my colleagues a while back and he's keen to stay in contact with you. He said if you need any help with your career going forward, this is his email address and telephone number." I took the phone number and put it into my phone so I could check out the profile picture. It was the journalist whom I'd met in the steam room. Mr BBC and Mr Journalist must be friends.

I replied to the email politely:"It was a pleasure to meet you too and thank you for the recording. Please tell your friend that, although it was nice to meet him, I don't feel we would benefit from meeting again. Regards, L.J." I didn't want him; I didn't want anyone other than Fox.

The kids were in their rooms pretending to do schoolwork with their Xboxes on, and I went about my daily planning for meals and housework so that I had free time in the evening to edit my book and reply to any requests from the publisher.

"Cough, cough." I spluttered, then stopped. Minutes later it started again,"Cough, cough, cough." I ran upstairs to the bathroom to get the first aid kit to take my temperature but couldn't find the thermometer. I caught my reflection in the mirror and yelped. There was a rash on my cheeks and my face was flushed."Oh, God, what do I do?" I talked to myself in the mirror. My thoughts went straight to the care of my children, and that I wouldn't be able to look after them if I was sick, and worst case, what if I died with them in the house?

I reached for the bleach and covered every surface I'd been near to eliminate germs, put a face mask on, and put all my clothes and any towels I'd used into the washing machine on a hot wash. I gathered some bottles of water out of the fridge, pain killers, and put them in a plastic bag, then carried them to my bedroom, shutting the door and locking it.

"Kids!" I shouted from my room.

"What, Mum?" my little boy answered me.

"I think I've got Covid. I've got what I need, and I've locked the door. You must try not to come in, so you don't get germs from me." My voice started to break as I knew how upset he would be.

"Mum, what's going on?" My daughter knocked at the door.

"You're going to have to look after your brother until I'm well enough to." I coughed out my words, nearly choking.

"Mum, you, okay? I'm worried." She started to sob.

"I'm just going to be a bit sick for a few days. I promise you I'll be okay. You have your dad's number; if things get bad, he'll have to come and get you, okay? Promise me you'll take good care of your brother for me?"

"I promise. I love you," she said, subdued.

"I love you too, Darling," I replied, breaking down. I'd never not been able to look after my own children before—it was the scariest moment of my life. I had no idea what was about to happen to me. I was burning up and getting worse by the minute. It'd come on so suddenly and hit me hard. I couldn't stop coughing; it was constant and debilitating.

I looked online for the NHS guidance on Covid symptoms:
· A high temperature or shivering (chills)—check
· A new, continuous cough—check
· A loss or change to your sense of smell or taste—not noticed.
· Shortness of breath—definitely
· Feeling tired or exhausted

The list went on, and I started to panic, which made my coughing worse."Oh, God, I'm going to die, alone and single! My poor kids!" I said, pathetically. I lay on my back and looked up at the celling, tears running down my face."What have I done to deserve this? Being alone sucks. I should have a partner, someone here to look after the kids while I'm sick." I sat up, looked at my reflection in the mirror, and noticed my face was bright red, my eyes bloodshot, and my vision was starting to go blurry, then my reflection split into two in front of my eyes.

I fell back onto my pillow and lay still."L.J.," a voice echoed around my room. I couldn't muster up the breath to answer, so I just blinked, washing hot tears down my face. I closed my eyes and started to doze.

"L.J., what are you doing in the mud? You'll get your dress all dirty."

"I'm making mud pies, Nanna, for our tea," I replied innocently, squishing mud through my fingers and patting around the sides to shape it. Dolly-Anna was sitting next to me with a set of teacups and plates; she went everywhere with me. Behind me was a berry tree. I got up and climbed the small wall to pick up some berries to put on top of the pies to make them look pretty.

"I'm a little teapot, short and stout. Here's my handle, here's my spout. I'm a very special teapot… Sing with me, Dolly-Anna. Would you like a mud pie? Nanna, tea's ready."

My heart pounded in my ears, and my body felt like it was moving, like sitting on a roller coaster backwards and being tugged and pulled. I looked at myself in the mirror again, only the reflection was of me with blonde hair and a camcorder in front of my face; I was dancing and filming myself, covered in paint. Artwork and canvases surrounded me, and The Music Children by Robert Miles was playing in the background. I was perfectly at peace. Happy thoughts surrounded me, then blackness for what seemed forever.

"Push L.J., one last push." The sound of a screaming baby filled the room."It's a girl." My beautiful baby was placed onto my chest in a towel, and I looked into her eyes.

"Look, she's looking right back at me!" My body started to feel like it was floating, like the wind was lifting me into the air.

"God, L.J., you poked me in the eye," Fox's voice mocked me as I wrapped myself around him, falling asleep in his arms. I felt safe and content—truly happy.

"Good night, Fox, I'm going to sleep now. I love you."

Suddenly, I was in the brightest light I've ever seen, like looking up at the sun when you're not supposed to. Warmth surrounded me, and

I walked toward outlines of people in the distance. It was strangely comforting, and I felt like I'd been here before, like I was coming home. I tripped and fell over something on the floor, and I sank, falling through the light into space and darkness.

"Where am I?" I screamed. I shot up, my sheets wet through with sweat. I was in my bed, in my home, and it was night-time.

"Mummy, Mummy, are you okay? I heard you scream." My little boy stood at the other side of my bedroom door.

"I'm fine, Darling, it was just a dream. Go back to bed." I turned my bedroom light on and looked all around me, now freezing and shivering.

"Did I just almost die? Why did I get sent back? Or was it just a dream?" I laid back down and covered myself with blankets, staring into space, my mind racing, recalling what'd just happened to me.

CHAPTER SEVENTEEN

"Pink Shoelaces" ~ Dodie Stevens

More time passed. I watched the world change around me. New rules, new restrictions, new order, until life as I knew it before would never be the same again. Covid had changed every aspect of how we went about our everyday lives. This did get progressively better, slowly but surely, we could go out again in public.

I picked up my water bottle ready for my daily run. I hadn't put my usual face of make-up on, just a dash to make sure I looked alive and healthy, not the hungover zombie I'd been since I last spoke to Fox.

I ran down my street, across the road, and onto the grass, wearing shades to stop anyone seeing my tired eyes, worn out from crying over Fox, and a cap to stop my hair getting in my face. I felt my ponytail blowing in the breeze as I ran. So many thoughts were in my head—I needed to give myself a good talking to. It wasn't like me to feel so down for so long. I was the queen of positivity. I could do anything. If I fell down, I got the f*ck back up. This had always been my way of dealing with things. I fought through life. I was a survivor.

So, what is it that he doesn't want? Why am I not good enough for him? My thoughts raced. What am I doing wrong? Does he not find me interesting? Am I not bright enough for him? Am I not attractive? Do I not tick all the boxes he needs me to tick? This is so frustrating! I thought we both felt the same. We get on so well, we have such AMAZING sex, so much in common, we talk all day, we laugh, we sing, we share everything with each other. I've never had a connection like it. Why is he not feeling what I feel? Does he not see something perfect?

Okay, so we don't live together, and he hasn't met my kids, but I've never introduced anyone to my children, no one's been important enough to me to risk that. I would like him to be part of that when he's ready, but I know he's not."Oh, my God, I'm going crazy." I ran faster and the breeze rushed, hitting my face, and I drank more water, feeling thirsty. Is this in my imagination? Am I really losing the plot? How can two people f*ck for so many years and not be going anywhere? Or have I set myself up for this by being so easy and available to him? I frowned at the realisation, my feet pounding into the ground as I felt myself getting more aggressively into my run.

I know he likes the sex; our sex is off the charts. Maybe that's why I can't give him up? Because I'm addicted to that and not really in love? I approached a tree and stood leaning against it to catch my breath. My head flooded with thoughts about what could possibly be wrong with me. But why should something be wrong with me? Maybe it's something that's wrong with him? He's mysterious at times and emotionally unavailable. I did a few stretches and then continued my route.

What does he mean by what he said? None of it makes any sense whatsoever. It's like he's talking in riddles. It should be so simple: boy meets girl, they want a relationship together, the end. Not boy meets girl, they f*ck, and that's it. That's what happened with Fancy Pants. It can't be happening to me again in a different way, can it? He seemed so into me! Could I have misread his body language? I've never been kissed that way by anyone—the passion. I've never wanted to have sex so much; well except for Fancy Pants, but that was different. He looked me in the eyes and connected with me. Is that not love? My ex-husband didn't look me in the eyes when we made love, not ever.

"Why am I questioning my own questions?" I felt my face burning with heat as I ran faster and faster, getting more and more frustrated with myself. He's my friend too; he talks to me and listens to me and gives me advice. He doesn't just f*ck me and then disappear like Fancy Pants did; there's a difference, a big difference. I wiped sweat off my face and felt a little dizzy. Exercise was new after I'd not been able to leave the house and had only sat down working.

So, he's my friend, my lover, and I adore him; why doesn't he feel the same way? What's stopping him from wanting to be in a happy, blissful relationship? Is he f*cked up? Is he lying to me? Is he emotionally challenged in some way? How the f*ck do I keep picking the same kind of guys?"When will a man actually like me back?" My eyes filled with tears; I was glad I was wearing my sunglasses to stop people staring.

I just want to be loved, not f*cked. I mean, I love sex, but I want to be loved and part of something more. Is this because of my books? Do men just think I'm a goodtime girl, an easy f*ck? I wish I'd never told him about the f*cking book, but then would he have even been interested in me? Apart from the books, what stands out about me? I checked my watch to see how much longer I had left to run and rolled my eyes; I felt like I'd been running forever.

I stopped to tie one of my pink shoelaces that had become loose, when my phone rang."Hello, L.J. speaking," I answered the call out of breath.

"Hello, L.J., it's your publisher here. We are ready for your manuscript for A Year of SINatra to be published. We love the work; just need your signature and agree on a date for release. I was so glad that my radio interview with the BBC was now not a complete embarrassment.

"Are you serious? That's amazing!" I shouted at the top of my voice.

"We loved it, L.J., it's a brilliant follow on. We can't wait to see the sales on this. Just remember, it's true to life, so no naming or shaming," she said, quite seriously.

"Fox, he's a very interesting character, isn't he?" She seemed to blush a little down the phone having read what we'd been up to in the bedroom.

"He's more than interesting!" I laughed down the phone.

"It's a very entertaining HOT and STEAMY read. We really do look forward to publishing this for you," she repeated herself.

"Excellent. We'll email you the release date options and the Trailor, then you need to read it as usual and check.

"Yes," I agreed." I stood and looked around at people staring and listening in on my conversation.

The first person I wanted to speak to was, of course, Fox to tell him I'd got another book out and that our sex life would be in print across the globe, but I thought better of it in my heightened state of emotion, so I dialled my friend and now fully committed editor, who never judged me and was always excited to work with me on the books.

"Hi, L.J.! How are you?" a friendly voice answered.

"You'll never guess what," I screamed down the phone.

"Go on," she said excitedly.

"I've got a release date coming soon for "A Year of SINatra!" I was talking way too loudly and jumping up and down on the spot like a lunatic.

"I knew you would," she said supportively. "It's a great story. I loved editing it." Aimee was like me, a divorcee and single mum. She had so much respect for what I was trying to achieve. We were singing off the same page in so many ways, and most important, we made a super team; we bounced off each other intellectually, and together we always found ways to tweak and improve my story. It helped that she was super-efficient and excellent at spelling and grammar, as I was useless at it. I wrote, and she corrected.

"It's going to be amazing, L.J.! Next year, we'll be having drinks at the Shard celebrating its success!" she said, with absolute confidence.

"I'm so excited! Thank you for being so supportive; you're the best!" I said lovingly, knowing how much effort she put into helping me.

"Have you told Fox?"

"Not yet, he's still suffering from after chemo." The moment became dark.

"I know you love him, but he's not treated you well. He needs to start making you a priority in his life and showing you that he really cares."

She was right, but it was hard to hear. I couldn't compute it in my head. It was like my brain was foggy. My heart said one thing, and my head told me another. Usually, they had a massive fight with each other, and we got nowhere fast.

"He's sick. I think he's the priority right now, not me." I put him before myself in my thoughts, and if I was honest with myself, I would be with him no matter how he treated me—it was unconditionally f*cked up.

"I don't know how I'm supposed to get him out of my head when I'm writing a book about our sex life—about being in love with him."

"Go and write, L.J.," she encouraged."Get it all out! Start another book!"

"Another book? I've only just finished this one."

"You've done incredibly well. You're a published author—it's awesome! You've still got so much to tell, though. Your story isn't finished. Keep pushing forward, keep learning, and keep writing!"

"Okay, I'll keep going." I started to run again."Never give up, right?"

"Yep, focus. Never give up. You've got this! Woo-hoo!" She hung up.

CHAPTER EIGHTEEN

"9PM (Till I Come)" ~ ATB

I wonder if all women wake up like me, horny and needing sex? It's every morning without fail, unless I'm sick or under a lot of stress, but even that sometimes doesn't get in the way. Either something's wrong with me or I'm perfectly normal and most women just don't talk about it. I closed my eyes and reached between my legs, trying to search in my head for who I wanted to have a fantasy about today. Fox? Nope, not today. Well, maybe later.

Jason Momoa? Oh my God, if I do, the roof of the house will blow off. What a sexy f*cking man! Jack Nicholson? He always gets a sneaky look in, the little devil. Fancy Pants? Nope, that's not it either. Maybe the sexy stranger? The guy I played eye tennis with at the supermarket last night? Hmm… yes… We hadn't touched and were wearing face masks, but felt the heat we created next to each other's trolleys in the queue at the checkout. He'd smelt so good, and he dressed well. I wonder what he'd look like naked.

I delved deep into my imagination and manifested an image of him, but my mind interrupted me, *Oi, L.J. What're you doing? Stop perving over strangers in supermarkets! Didn't your parents tell you about stranger danger? Actually, I take that back. I read your first book; you're a liability!* an Irish voice echoed in my ears.

"Mr Belfast?" I was alarmed."What are you doing in my head?"

It's your imagination, L.J.… You need to get a plastic sheet fitted, save your mattress any more damage. It's taken quite a hit already.

"You're just as bad as Fancy Pants for intruding. I want to think about the man in the supermarket, thanks. So politely sod off."

Oh, I'm here too, L.J. Fancy Pants' voice bellowed, then laughed.

We all are, L.J. Fox's voice now, and he sounded quite displeased at the situation.

"Fox, I wasn't cheating on you, I just liked the look of this guy and he smelt of your aftershave. You're not around, and I need to feel sexy, with or without you."

We're watching you trying to make yourself cum.

"Well, go away, this is my private time. I don't watch you!" They all laughed, and I realised I'd watched all three of them at some point play and explode in front of me.

"Okay, fair enough, but not all at the same time. Give me a break. I'm trying to concentrate on one person."

Ha ha… yeah, right, said Fancy Pants. No one only thinks about one person. We all look; it's in our genes. We all watch porn, and we all have fantasies.

Look, can you all go away? I'm trying to enjoy a little bit of me time, and you're distracting me!" It fell silent and I was glad they'd gone. I slid my hand back down between my legs and started to play.

Look at that technique, said Fancy Pants.

She's incredible, isn't she? Fox replied proudly.

I taught her, said Fancy Pants.

I think you'll find she taught herself, Fox snapped back.

I got to watch once. Mr Belfast added like a giddy child.

"Oh, will you guys just STOP? I'm trying to CUM here!" They all apologised one by one, and it went silent again, so I continued to play, slowing building to an orgasm. I screamed out my first, then my second.

Bravo! I got a round of applause from them all as they watched me fall apart.

"Guys, stop being such perverts! Haven't you got anything better to do?"

I have to polish the Porsche, said Fancy Pants, but this is way more entertaining.

I'm going to have to play with myself later, said Fox.

I'm going to f*ck you again one day, said Mr Belfast.

"Oh, are you now? Bit far away to do that, aren't you? Why don't you all go help Fancy Pants polish his precious car and let me get on with what I'm doing?"

Ah, come on, L.J., we all love to make you cum. Just relax and go with the flow. We can all give you something different to lust over and you know it.

A foursome! shouted Fancy Pants. Let's have a pleasure party! he continued.

"Fancy Pants, you're over dominating the situation; you might as well have peed all around me to mark your territory!"

Well then, kick the other two out of your head and let's get it on. I'll sing New York, New York to you again. Kick them out of your head. You know I'm the one.

You're not her one, replied Fox, snapping at Fancy Pants. I am.

"Fox, are you serious? You've never said that before." They argued between themselves, fighting for my affection, until the confusion became too much."Okay, look, let's settle this fairly with a quiz. The winner takes all—me."

"What is the world record for the most female orgasms recorded?" I waited with anticipation."No phones allowed," I stressed.

Is it you, said Mr Belfast. He creased himself with laughter but was quite serious at the same time.

"No, it's not me." I rolled my eyes."Any ideas?" I looked at them for a guess at the very least.

Two hundred and fifty? Fancy Pants answered.

"Any more guesses, guys?" They shook their heads in defeat."One hundred and thirty-four." I felt slightly jealous."Let's not draw this out. Three questions for three contestants. Winner gets me and the rest of you have to leave my head, okay? How do you have great sex? Is it, 'A,' connection, 'B,' loving your own body, 'C,' exploring new things, or 'D,' being in love?"

Sex is enough, replied Fancy Pants.

Connection, said Mr Belfast.

A through to C, said Fox.

"One point to Fox, nil to Fancy Pants, and one point to Mr Belfast!"

I'm not playing any more. This is boring me. I'm going, said Fancy Pants. He had his usual tantrum, then disappeared.

"Last question, winner takes all. What's the sexiest thing about a woman? 'A,' confidence, 'B,' intelligence, 'C,' what she looks like, or 'D,' a sense of humour?"

Tits and ass, shouted Mr Belfast. C.

If a woman is sexy, it's because you like all the things about her, 'A' through to 'D.'

"Point to Fox, and he's the winner," I said proudly, with relief.

Mr Belfast, with all due respect, I'm older than you, and I've been sleeping with L.J. for years. You have no idea who she is or how to satisfy her, so just be a good fella and jump out of the game so I can please make her cum. He was extremely polite.

"Do you always win, Fox?"

With you, yes. In life, not always.

"No one else is ever going to make me cum again other than you, are they?"

Not if I have anything to do with it. Why do you still think about those guys, anyway? They don't care about you.

"Only people I've had good sex with, I guess, other than you. They're in the jill till."

Close your eyes and let me make you cum, you f*cking nutter!

"I miss you so much! I need you to get better. I need you to come back to me!"

CHAPTER NINETEEN

"Stuck on a Feeling" ~ Prince Royce

After such a long time without hearing from Fox, I got a text asking me to make myself free for a visit. Like he'd promised, he'd come back to me. He'd survived his treatment, and today was the day I'd get to see him again.

Having not seen him for over a year, he was going to be at my house in a matter of minutes. I was fixed to the spot, staring at my phone on the kitchen work surface. Looking up, I saw my reflection staring back fearfully in the cooker splashback. My body was filled with anxiety, my heart racing.

The door opened without him introducing himself, but that didn't surprise me. I heard slow footsteps approach the kitchen, and my body started to shake nervously. I turned around slowly and leant against the worktop to steady myself. He wore a face covering, but his eyes told me that he was smirking behind it. The burning eyes that'd danced with my soul, torn me apart, and sent me insane were unchanged, though his body was completely different.

He stopped in his tracks, stood in front of me, and slowly pulled off his face mask."The face mask was a joke." He tried to lighten the atmosphere between us. He was thin and frail, a different version of himself. His eyes were sunken and looked bruised, his beard thick, wiry, and out of control, not clean shaven. He looked ill, old, and extremely tired from the cancer that'd tried to ravage his body. He was dressed in a grey sweatshirt and deep blue shorts to match his tired eyes. His legs and arms were thinner than mine, and his clothes hung off him.

I took one step toward him, lifted my hand to slap him, but pulled back. I couldn't hurt him."Why the f*ck did you leave me to deal with this alone? I've been going out of my mind with worry!" I cried out, my voice breaking with emotion and tears falling down my face. I was breathing hard and exhaling fast, feeling dizzy and out of control, scared of what I'd almost done to him and how much it could have hurt his fragile body.

"I've been in hell, L.J.," he replied calmly, knowing he'd have deserved a slap."It's nice to see you too," he said, now slightly amused.

"You just left me, in a pandemic! You disappeared without any communication when you were so sick. After our last call. I thought you'd died! You let me believe you were dead! Can you imagine what that did to me? I told you that I loved you, Fox!" I spat out my words in frustration.

"It is what it is. You're looking very well," he said, likely expecting me to be flattered. It worked, even though I was overwhelmed by confusion.

"You look like sh*t," I said without thinking, choking my words out, putting my hand over my mouth with regret."Is your treatment over now?" I questioned, gently twiddling my fingers in his beard, then running them down toward his neck where I could see the scar from the operation on his pale skin.

"I'm in remission," he said with confidence."I promised myself that you'd be the first person I'd see once I was well enough. I made it one of my goals to keep me going. I didn't want you to see me going through chemo." He stepped closer and put his hands around my waist.

"I would've been there for you every day." My lip quivered and tears poured down my face at the thought of him being so sick, his strong character and frame being made weak and helpless.

"I had people to support me." He looked away.

"So, I didn't fit into the equation?" I said coldly, instantly feeling guilt and jealousy that I was so irrelevant.

"L.J., I know you probably better than anyone in the world. You wouldn't have been able to handle it. You're too soft." He wiped away my tears and we stared into each other's eyes painfully. He moved closer, grabbing the back of my neck tightly, pulling me to his face. He leaned into me and kissed me so hard my lip started to bleed, biting my tongue, and kissing my neck passionately like his life depended on it.

His mouth tasted different and felt dry, slightly sticky, and it surprised me, but I couldn't get away from his grip. He had me pinned against the worktop as he wildly ripped my dress apart and pushed my panties to the floor while continuing to kiss me.

"Fox, I'm cumming," I shouted in alarm as I suddenly became very wet, and his shorts became a darker shade of blue. My head went dizzy from the passionate kiss, and I felt like I was going to faint.

"But… I haven't touched you." He put his hand across his mouth in disbelief, his eyes wide."I've just made you cum by kissing you?" He was stunned.

"I guess so. Either that or I've become incontinent!" I looked at him equally as concerned, then started to giggle nervously. He dropped his shorts to the floor, revealing his hard cock, lifted me up onto the work top, opened my legs, and pushed himself inside me effortlessly. I gasped at the intensity and threw my head back so he could kiss my neck.

He bit my breasts and skin and pushed hard and fast before pulling out of me slowly and placing his fingers deep inside me instead. I closed my eyes and bit my bleeding lip. I pulled my hand through my hair and slowly down my face, placing my finger in my mouth to wipe the blood away.

"Fox, something's different when you kiss me. I mean, it's still amazing, but it's not as lubricated. Is it the illness? What else do I need to expect?"

"It's dry mouth. It happens after chemo. I have to drink a lot of water. It feels sticky, right? I'm sorry." He seemed slightly embarrassed. I kissed him and held his face, looking into his eyes.

"Just tell me everything I need to know, and we'll work through this together. I'm not scared."

"L.J., I saw the shock on your face when I walked in the room. I've lost a lot of weight, almost three stone. I don't know if I'll ever put it back on again, either. Does that bother you?" He searched me for an answer.

"I didn't get with you for your looks; I fell for you because of who you are as a person, Fox. So, no, it doesn't bother me." I cuddled into him for warmth, and he squeezed me tightly.

"L.J., I'm taking you to bed!" He confidently pulled me up the short staircase, even in his fragile state, and threw me onto my bed. Closing the door behind him, he pulled his top over his head and tossed it onto the floor in a heap. His tall body stood over me in dominance. I now saw how sick he'd really been; I'd never seen his ribs before. His body had completely changed, apart from his penis, which had luckily escaped without damage. My mind rushed with emotion and worry, but, above all, irrevocable love for him. It didn't matter what he looked like, where he'd been, what he'd done, or why he'd left me—I was glad he wasn't a ghost and that he'd been spared.

"What else has changed, Fox?" I said, carefully and softly, watching him undress. "Will I hurt you if we have sex?"

"Just try not to touch my neck. It still gets very sore. It pulls and effects my ear. Also, I get tired quickly, so I might not be able to go for as long as we usually do without having a nap in-between. I sleep a lot, even in the day now. My main worry is keeping a hardon for you. If this doesn't work, I might as well be dead," he jested. "Everything has changed, L.J. I'm not the man I was before."

"I'm so sorry, Fox. I had no idea." I felt so sad.

"Food is another thing. I can't swallow very well. I've been eating soups and things that will slide down my throat with ease. I would kill for a steak!" He was open and vulnerable with me, and it brought tears to my eyes knowing what he'd gone through and how much it'd changed him. "I need to drink water all the time, too. In fact, could you go grab some for me so I can take some Viagra?" He took a packet out of his pocket and threw them on the bed. I did as I was told and hurried back to him.

"I've taken two," he said, swigging some water, then diving down between my legs and pulling them apart as far as he could without hurting me. He looked up at me with heat in his eyes, making me moan instantly.

"God, I've missed this." He put his fingers inside me, making me cry out.

"I've missed it too!" I reached for his hand and held it tightly. He slid inside me, and we were face to face, looking into each other's eyes, then he suddenly stopped.

"Are you okay?" I looked surprised.

"L.J., I'm so sorry. Nothing like this has happened to me before." He looked disappointed.

"What is it?" I felt worried.

"I've cum." He laid his head on my stomach to rest.

"Oh, well, that's a good thing!" I tried to be positive."At least you know you still can!" He raised his head and shook it in disbelief, turning onto his back."Just give me a few minutes and we can try again," he insisted.

"Don't put yourself under any pressure. It's fine." I kissed his cheek and laid next to him.

"So, what's happening with the books?" He changed the subject.

"Well, I have a photoshoot on Monday, and the second book's out in a month… I'm a busy girl! Thinking of what to put in the third one now. What with the pandemic, it's all been pretty boring." My mind went back to seeing him throw away my manuscript, but it wasn't the right time to bring the subject up.

"I'm sleeping with a celeb, one who writes porn, and who I can make cum by kissing," he replied playfully.

"I'm sleeping with a hero." I turned to him, and his face was flushed from the tablets he'd taken. He grabbed my hand and put it on his cock.

"We have lift off." He grinned and pulled me on top of him.

"Let's f*ck, shall we?" He pounded into me, and I yelped in pleasure.

"YEE-HAW! Let's ride this, cowboy!" I laughed and he did too… and like it was yesterday, we were back to being one again, completely lost in the moment.

CHAPTER TWENTY

"Train Wreck" ~ James Arthur

A few weeks after we were reunited, he ended it again. His excuse was his illness. This rollercoaster of ours was out of control. Friends and family tried to pull me out of my despair:

"You'll get over it."

"You need to move on."

"Just forget about him."

Nothing anyone said helped the way my heart felt about the situation. My head was not participating. This was all about how I felt emotionally. I thought about him all the time. The pain I felt was with me all the time. I was irrational, distracted, over-emotional, and most evenings, drunk. I barely recognised myself. And for what? A man who didn't even love me back. It was a ridiculous situation. It didn't make any sense to me or anyone else around me. I desperately wanted to find a solution.

Make yourself busy, throw yourself into work, get a hobby, take it out on the gym were suggestions I received on how to get over heartache and move on. I'd tried them all, and they failed. I was a mess. Nothing anyone said, helped me even slightly. Train wreck was an understatement. I couldn't eat, I couldn't sleep, and I couldn't stop crying. I had anxiety, I was depressed, and I was drinking heavily. What if I never get over this? I thought in complete despair.

I scrolled through his Facebook, looking at photos of him, desperate to know what he was doing while he wasn't talking to me or with me anymore. I was jealous, paranoid, and I stopped looking after myself. I completely let myself go; I wasn't smartly dressed any more, I put on weight because of the wine, my hair was awful, and I had big bags under my eyes. I was unrecognisable to myself when I looked in the mirror. I'd hit rock bottom.

I checked my phone every hour to see if I'd been unblocked, he'd sent an email, or reached out in anyway. I longed for some indication that he felt just as lost without me, but I received nothing.

Every day I listened to YouTube videos, Ted Talks, and advice about how to get over a broken heart and heal from unrequited love. Most of them said the same thing,"time is a great healer," and to be patient with the process.

I watched the international love guru repeatedly and read, How to Get the Guy, which left me crying because he was right about most things he said; I just couldn't bring myself to accept it. I even got angry with him for telling the truth, virtually giving Hussey the finger. I tried to act like it was all a walk in the park, but it wasn't. Inside my heart and mind, it was a living hell.

Guy Winch, who was now one of my favourite go-tos, helped me stay sane and made intellectual sense of the situation. When I was drinking and felt like I was full of attitude, Russell Brand's talks on love were direct and punched the feelings right where they needed to be. I scrolled through the internet looking for answers, for someone to strike a chord that was familiar and who made things make sense again.

Talks on love, divorce, self-esteem, mental health disorders linked to break ups, addiction, relationship crisis, childhood, and the effects it has on our adult relationships, co-dependency, loss and grief, the cycles of abuse in relationships, self-destruction, self-sabotage, how to be happy, how to be alone, how not to be alone, sex addiction, counselling for couples, endless crappy love songs, and the f*cking holy Bible. I put myself through endless torture searching for answers as to why I was so deeply lost after this breakup.

"F*cking pointless internet is full of sh*t." I pushed my laptop to one side, and it fell off the bed onto the floor. The laptop had fallen keys down, and it'd randomly selected some relationship expert I'd never come across before. She started to talk, and my attention was heightened. What happened next was a lifeline.

Her name was Esther Perel, and she was brutally honest and open-minded, like me. Her words and her approach took me by surprise. She talked of how death and mortality often live in the shadow of a relationship breakdown and that growth and self-discovery can come from it. It felt like something resonated with me, the words she said.

What was missing from the relationship? Not passion, sexual connection, or mind connection; we could talk about things we would never in a million years discuss with anyone else. We'd been intellectually, physically, emotionally, and sexually hooked. It all worked, apart from commitment, and not for want of me trying. Fox and I were best friends, playful, and had the same wanderlust in life, both dreaming about the next big adventure, and what could excite us. He definitely got a big kick out of being with me. So, what was he holding back for? Why was he pushing me away?

He always said that when he was with me, he felt so alive, and I saw it in his eyes. He was on fire, not just with lust but with simply allowing himself to be the 'real' him. What he was doing with me was trying not to let himself die inside. The conflict between his boundaries and his behaviour were what constantly made us swing from one extreme to the other. He missed me and he pulled me back, and we went around in circles.

I'd been consistent. We had the biggest fights I'd ever had with a partner, then we made up and had incredible 'make up sex.' It always left me in limbo, in some dark place between heaven and hell. I loved him so much, and I wanted him to see what we could be, how we could have a better life if we were together. He was just unavailable to me.

He'd told me he had a nice house, nice things, and plenty of money. I was the opposite, a single mum with a constant overdraft and no savings. I knew that would change eventually—when my books became popular. I told him how I wanted to buy a farmhouse, do it up, and build a tree house shag pad for us, where we could look at the stars together. I had a plan. I could see our future. I could even see marriage. But what was he seeing?

No wonder I was going insane! This level of emotional instability was not sustainable. It was unhealthy, and enough to drive anyone mad. What was he hiding his feelings for? I tried thinking about it from his perspective without really understanding him or even knowing if what he was telling me was the truth. So much was hidden that this was virtually impossible. It felt like a dead end, like there was nothing I could do to pull this back or make it any different.

I couldn't help thinking that I'd caused my own loneliness. If I'd not given him all of me, perhaps this would have been another story? But I'd found it impossible. I'd bared my soul to him because it felt natural.

I shouldn't wait for someone who never shows up for me, though, should I? Or would he be worth the wait?

I was heartbroken and going insane because the only solution was to walk away from someone who made me feel like no one had ever made me feel. It felt like I would no longer be a whole person somehow. I couldn't remember how it felt to be the person I was before, though I'm sure I was a little happier, carefree even, and life wasn't as heavy.

I needed a distraction, something to take my mind away from him and help me feel sexy and wanted again. Mr Belfast had reached out again for the promised second meeting. Maybe I should give him another chance? He did say that we were the same person split in two. I'd plan a trip to Belfast and have something to look forward to.

CHAPTER TWENTY-ONE

"You'll Never Walk Alone" ~ Gerry & The Pacemakers

Fox had spent his entire life in Liverpool. He'd sent me so many photos of football matches he'd attended here, showing off his VIP lifestyle, when I couldn't even afford to eat. I found it ironic that I'd never been to the centre, only the outskirts once, the day I met him at the haunted house. Today, I'd been forced to this unfortunate destination on passport duty so I could fly to see Mr Belfast. The city was vast and busy, and I knew immediately that a city life wouldn't work for me. I'd never been to a city and felt this uncomfortable before.

I walked out of the centre to the water's edge, found a bench, and sat looking out over the river Mersey. I felt like I really didn't belong anywhere near him or his hometown."So, this is where you grew up?" I said out loud, not thinking about passers-by who looked at me as if I were a person of mental inadequacy. I closed my mouth and people watched as thoughts about my years with Fox raced through my mind. He was right when he said that I'd never survive living in Liverpool, so we'd never live together as he refused to ever move.

I looked at the water glistening in the sunlight and admired the beauty of what surrounded the city. I'd text him to let him know I was in his neighbourhood, but he'd replied with,"I'm busy working." I sat by the water looking out for what seemed forever, thinking about him and what'd happened to us. I was so close to him, yet he made so little effort to see me. I'd started to accept this was his normal behaviour. My memories and flashbacks of us reverted right back to the beginning, to try to make some sense of our unrequited love affair.

March 2019

Shall we get the stairs or the elevator?" He watched me take one last gulp of wine, and I instructed him with my eyes as I got up from the bar stool and staggered toward the elevator. I stepped in and slumped against the mirrored wall, seeing my refection many times and giggling.

"Which one are you going to kiss first, Fox?" I pointed all around me, giving out a wine-induced laugh.

"I think I have my hands full with this one." He held my face and pinned me to a corner of the elevator, looking into my eyes for permission as he touched my lips for the first time and kissed me passionately.

"Oh, God, wow," I spoke into his mouth."Is this a Liverpool thing? Where did you learn to kiss like that?" I pressed the buttons to go back down.

"What've you done that for?" He looked at me puzzled."Have you forgotten something in the bar?"

"No, I just want you to do that again." I kissed him back as the elevator took us back up to his room.

Six months later, we were calling each other every second of the day. I'd never felt so happy and in love in all my life. It seemed the perfect relationship. We had everything: trust, lust, and fun. We were invincible, until the day he found out about Mr Belfast.

"What's your problem? We'd been together a week!" I screamed down the phone in tears."It was a one-night stand. I was drunk. I didn't even need to tell you. I could have f*cking lied. He contacted my publisher, I didn't look him up, I didn't even have his number. It's been years!" I begged forgiveness hysterically down the phone."I love you, please don't go, don't leave me. We have such a great thing. Our book's going to be published soon, read it, and see how much I f*cking love you," I pleaded desperately.

"The Irish guy will always come between us," he snapped."I knew what'd happened before you told me; you're a terrible liar." He was unemotional and distracted.

"I'm so sorry! I didn't understand what I felt for you, or Fancy Pants, and we just randomly met. It was just a one-night stand; I didn't plan it. I won't see him ever again. It's you and no one else forever. I love you like I love my family. I'm so sorry." I was broken and felt so incredibly remorseful.

"I've never told you what to do or how to live your life. I've got another call. I need to go." After that conversation, we were never the same. My head filled with so many emotions and what ifs, and I blamed myself for him not loving me.

I looked out at the Mersey and rubbed the tears away from my eyes. Opening my bag, I found a sandwich and drink I'd brought with me. Taking them out, a man sat next to me on the bench."Hello, are you okay?" The stranger noticed my tear-filled eyes and my mascara running. He was older than me, not very well dressed, and smelt of alcohol. He had kind eyes, and you could tell he'd been having a hard time; he looked like he'd been sleeping rough.

"No, not really." I broke down, stuffing the sandwich into my mouth."Do you want some?" I offered my food to him, but his hands gestured 'no.'

He pulled out a bottle of vodka from his bag."Do you want some?" He looked at me sympathetically. I took the bottle from him and swigged the cold strong liquid.

"Thank you, I needed that." I smiled and tossed my sandwich into the water, watching seagulls dive on it almost immediately.

"So, what's your story?" he asked in a thick Liverpudlian accent.

"Broken heart." I shook my head as the vodka hit me."Years of a f*cked-up relationship, and I've lost my mind. I've gone insane over a guy who doesn't even want me," I said truthfully.

"My heart's broken too." He passed me back the vodka."Well, not quite the same. My wife died. I've been drunk ever since." I looked at the man, shocked.

"I'm so sorry for your loss." He nodded but didn't say a word.

"I come here because it's where we last sat together, looking out over the Mersey." He took another swig from his bottle, then offered it back.

"No, I'm okay, thank you." We both stared out again to the water and were silent.

"So, what's your tragic love story?" He cheered up a little and searched for his cigarettes.

"Oh, it's nothing like yours. He just doesn't love me." My eyes filled with sadness.

"There are all types of loss. Yours is just different to mine. Are you sure you loved him? It wasn't just a crush?"

Did I love him? I was as sure of the feeling as the sun sets and rises."Everything about him made me love him, and the more I got to know him, the deeper I fell in love with him. The way he walked, talked, smelled; how it felt to touch him, to kiss him, and how he made me laugh." I closed my eyes as the pain hit me."But it's all in my head. He's an imaginary boyfriend. He never loved me back, not for one second—I just hoped he would one day. I held on to that hope for nearly four years and even wrote two books about him."

"You're published?" He looked at me excitedly.

"Yes, L.J. Brown in the flesh. It's nice to meet you." I shook his hand and giggled."But I'm poor, I've made nothing—might never do." I shrugged.

"So, you've written about love?" he continued to question me.

"I've written about f*cking, mixed with love. A true story, not fiction."

"How could he not want you? What's wrong with the man?"

"Oh, he wants me, but he wants me for one thing: our incredible sex life." I blushed as his mouth stayed open in disbelief."It's my own fault, really. He's repeatedly said he never wanted anything serious, just our fun times. I didn't listen to him, so I've caused some of my own pain. I didn't see the warning signs either, or I guess I was love blind and chose to ignore them, but he didn't always talk to me nicely or treat me well." My mind went back to a day he'd been particularly horrible…

"F*ck, it's stuck, I can't get it out of the mud!" He started to panic while trying to get out of the car and observing the wheel firmly stuck.

"Oh no, let me try and help," I giggled, finding the situation slightly amusing.

"How are you finding this funny?" he shouted at me harshly."I have to get back to Liverpool for my appointment, the car's stuck in the mud, and we're in the middle of nowhere. L.J., sometimes you're such a child," he continued aggressively.

"Don't speak to me like that. It's not my fault we're stuck in the mud. You wanted to go for a drive so you could feel me up and f*ck me." I got back into the car and slammed the door in anger. I watched him flag down a tractor and ask for help. While they assessed the situation, another car stopped, and a couple got out. You could clearly see they knew what we'd been up to.

He came back to the car, opened the door, and said firmly,"Stay inside the car. They're going to pull it out of the mud with a rope." I ignored him, my face still mad with anger at how he continued to talk to me. When the car was out, he got back in and drove off at speed, thanking the other people as we drove past them.

He drove in silence for a while then came to a dead-end near a field. He parked and turned to me."Get in the back," he ordered.

"No," I snapped and crossed my arms. Before I knew it, he launched across the car and kissed me hard.

"Suck my cock," he ordered me, putting his hand between my legs and starting to get me wet. I opened the car door and got in the back; he did the same.

"What if someone sees us?" I looked around nervously.

"We're in the middle of nowhere, L.J. No one will see us." He pulled off my panties and went down on me, making me moan. I'd again fallen under his spell. I couldn't resist him. He knew exactly what to do to control me, so I'd do whatever he wanted me to.

"Sh*t, it's a car," I yelped at the chance of getting caught. He looked at me and out of the back window.

"You're not going to believe this. It's the couple who helped us out of the mud. Get dressed, quick." I giggled to myself at the memory…

"It wasn't all bad; we had some incredible times together," I said, turning to the man next to me on the bench. He'd fallen asleep. I sighed and took a deep breath, gathered my things, and looked for my purse."Get some food and sober up. There's always hope, and you might meet someone else," I said softly, putting a 20-pound note in his jacket pocket before walking away.

I strolled along the Mersey, thinking about our best bits, but realised that all the best times had revolved around sex. We'd never spent any time doing anything other than sex. Although I'd thought about him when I watched a sunset, I'd never actually seen a sunset with him. Right now, I might be walking where he'd walked, but we never went for a long walk together, and he wouldn't hold my hand or talk to me about his day, like I see so many couples doing.

Why did I still want him so much? Still long for him? Why did I love him so much when he didn't love me back? Why couldn't I just walk away and be grateful I'd met him? I'm his love junkie; I'm addicted to him. He's my own brand of heroin, and I don't know if I can ever beat the habit or let go of him.

One thing was for sure, I was going to Belfast, and I was going to try to move forward.

CHAPTER TWENTY-TWO

"Around the World" ~ Daft Punk

We'd come out of our second lockdown, and life was slowly returning to normal again. I'd been distracting myself from the pain and misery of knowing that Fox no longer wanted me, with Mr Belfast. I still had bad days when I'd drink, get emotional, and miss Fox, and the idea of us being together, but I tried my best to move away from it—from him. I felt guilty talking to someone else, but I forced myself to. I had to try and find peace and happiness.

Mr Belfast and I'd messaged a few times until the early hours of the morning, reflected on the night we'd spent together years ago, and how much we wanted to do it again. And I'd written him naughty love letters. It was a nice distraction. He was straight-forward and easy to talk to. Everything was black and white. Texting all the time was hard though, as we never really got any depth to our conversations—it all seemed surface level, even though we lusted for one another.

Finally, we arranged a date. I offered to fly to Belfast to meet him, instead of him coming to Yorkshire, because he had a young child, so getting time away was a challenge."I'm on my way to the airport," I called, leaving him a voicemail, and knowing he was at work until the evening when we were supposed to meet. I didn't expect a response as he never picked up his phone in work hours. Minutes later, though, I received a text, which surprised me somewhat.

"My sister's fallen and broken her leg, and my mum's on holiday, so my childcare for tonight is no longer available. I'm doing my best to find someone else to fill in for me here. Don't worry, I'll sort it." He sent a photo of her leg in plaster, and I frowned.

"Oh no, your poor sister! Okay, well, keep me posted. I board the plane in two hours." I felt nervous. I'd not been on a plane since my marriage, and even then, I'd had to be sedated because I hated flying so much—the fear of not being in control. I was doing this for two reasons: one, I needed to get laid as I hadn't had sex in such a long time and I wanted good sex; and two, he was this mysterious man who kept chasing me, and I felt like I owed it to him to give him a chance. Even though I knew I wasn't ready, I pushed myself into it. This was my next big step: sleep with someone else.

I went through all the security checks, which with everyone wearing face masks was a strange experience. I was now filled with a mixture of dread and excitement about seeing him when he met me at the airport. Five years has got to change a person, right? I wonder if he's shaved. In his last few selfies, he looked like Grizzly Adams. No way I would be able to cope with him going down on me with that amount of hair tickling between my legs. I chuckled as I walked into the departure lounge and headed toward the bar.

What if he doesn't fancy me as much? I'm blonde and I was dark last time we met. What if he thinks I'm fat? I've put weight on since we saw each other. I ordered a drink at the bar and downed it, my hand shaking with fear of getting on the plane. "I'll have another large glass of Merlot please, and a shot of tequila," I ordered politely to the bartender.

"Fear of flying?" He looked at me knowingly.

"How could you tell?" I threw back the tequila and nodded to him that he was right.

"We get it a lot. You'd be surprised how many people are terrified of getting on a plane," he said, slightly amused by me.

"Well, it's not just that actually. I'm going on a date with a guy I've not seen for five years." I sucked the lemon and screwed my face up with the bitter taste.

"Well, that's something I don't hear a lot. He must be really special to get a girl to fly to him." He looked me up and down and smiled sympathetically.

"He would have come to me; it's just I had the time and money, and he had an issue with childcare," I said factually and convincingly.

"Well, I hope it works out for you. How did you meet?"

"At a ball, across a bar." I blushed and recalled the instant connection and warmth I felt at the memory.

"Love at first sight?" he continued.

"Kind of, yes. It was like magic." I blushed further and sipped my wine, one eye on the board looking for my plane details.

"Then what happened?" He seemed overly interested in my story.

"We spent the night together and had the best sex of my life—until then, at least." The wine had now gone to my head.

"Wow, I didn't expect you to be so honest." He looked at me in amazement.

"I've just had a full glass of wine and a shot in five minutes. I don't think I'd be able to do anything but tell the truth right now. Anyway, why be dull or lie to tell a socially acceptable story?" I snapped slightly and he backed off.

"So, you've just been talking for five years?" He looked astonished at my unique situation.

"No, I'm a writer, and he tracked me down through my publisher. I was with someone at the time so rejected him. When that guy dumped me, it was the perfect time to reconnect."

"You are? Have I heard of you?" He looked starstruck at me.

"I've only been writing for six years, and I'm not famous." I made it out to be no big deal.

"You're going to marry this man, I think," he said, smiling from ear to ear.

"That'd be nice. He's a great guy. Fate is in play, I think." I listened as my flight was being called, drank the last of the wine, and felt slightly sick but drunk enough to deal with the flight now.

"Belfast international now boarding," the intercom sounded out into the airport.

"Thanks for the drinks and the chat!" I put my glass down and picked up my bag.

"Good luck." He waved as I dashed away from the bar.

Getting on the plane, my heart started to race. I had a window seat right next to the wing and sat down immediately and put my seat belt on. Fixed to the spot, I closed my eyes and thought about seeing him at the other side: the warm embrace, the reassuring hug, the epic, long-anticipated kiss. All that got me through the flight. Well, that and another glass of wine.

When we touched down, I exited the plane and headed for the toilet to make sure I looked good when I saw him. I turned on my phone and had a few messages. Smiling excitedly, I expected one to say,"I'm here waiting for you." Instead, I read,"L.J., I'm really struggling to find someone to have my little boy. I'm asking everyone I know." I felt the stress he was under from the text, so I tried to call him, but got his voicemail.

"So, you're not picking me up from the airport now?" I texted, full of disappointment.

"You'll have to get a taxi to the hotel, and I'll meet you there."

"Okay, well I'll see you soon then I guess. You have to put your boy first." I started to feel a little bit cross at how disorganised he'd been. He'd had several weeks' notice that I was coming to Belfast. I kept my hopes high, though, that it would magically work out somehow.

I flagged a taxi down and got in."Where to, Miss?" the driver asked in a thick Belfast accent.

"The Titanic Hotel, please. Do you need the address?" I reached inside my bag for the details.

"No need, I know it well." He looked at me in amusement.

"So, what brings you to Ireland?" He struck up polite conversation; he'd obviously picked up on the worry on my face.

"I'm on a date, I think." I shrugged, not really knowing what to say.

"You've flown from where?" he continued to question me.

"Liverpool, but I don't live there, I live in Yorkshire." I looked down at my hands and started to fidget. My mood had dropped.

"That's a long way to go on a date! I hope he's paying." He looked at me shocked.

"No, I've paid for everything myself, including a hotel and dinner." I bit my lip and looked out of the window, feeling like an idiot.

"Well, you must really like him then," he continued, then fell silent and put the radio on. The song Belle of Belfast City was playing, and it made me smile and raised my spirits slightly. I loved this song; it made me want to dance."We're a few minutes away from the hotel. I'll help you with your bags." I thanked him as we pulled up outside. It was beautiful, very posh, and authentic. I don't think I'd ever stayed in a hotel as fancy. I recalled the memories of organising the booking with Mr Belfast, the excitement around it, and what we were going to do to each other when we got naked. I closed my eyes and imagined him, wishing for a miracle so he could make it.

The Titanic's white star was on the floor of the reception. It was incredible. I imagined the original building, the rooms where the Titanic had been designed and the people who must've passed in and out of here never to return from their fateful journey. All of a sudden, I felt proud and privileged to be in such a wonderful, historic hotel. I checked in and walked through the poorly lit corridors to my room, which looked like it belonged on a ship. I opened the door and looked around; it was beautiful! There were rose petals on the bed and champagne on ice with two glasses—the perfect romantic scene.

I went to the bathroom to freshen up when my phone beeped with a message; I ran across the room to read it excitedly. It was him:"I'm really sorry, L.J. I've tried everything, and I can't get anyone to watch my son. I won't be coming." I was in shock. For a few minutes I didn't know how to reply to him. Should I be angry, sad, or sympathetic?

"I can't believe this. I've just flown all this way to be stood up?" I went down the fumingly angry path without being able to hold back.

"So much for, 'put your boy first,'" he snapped back.

"We've had this planned for weeks. Hire a nanny, they're qualified to do it." Put some effort into this, I thought.

"I'm not leaving my son with a stranger just for a shag," he continued.

"OH, SO I'M JUST A SHAG NOW, AM I?" I texted in capitals.

"YOU'RE A SPOILT BRAT, THAT'S WHAT YOU ARE!" he texted back in capitals.

"I'm perfectly within my rights to be a little pissed off right now." I started to cry, then tried to call him, but he hung up.

"Look, I tried. It can't be helped. Enjoy your night. Go into Belfast."

"I think you're telling me lies. Are you in a relationship? Because this doesn't add up." I walked to the champagne bottle and popped the cork, taking a swig from the cold bottle."There's rose petals on the bed, champagne, the works—for us. I've put so much effort into this. I'm mad with you."

"Look, like I said. I told you I would try my best, but never said for definite I would be able to make it."

"Then why did you even let me fly over here in the first place? It's outrageous. I'd never do this to anyone, ever. I thought you liked me?"

"Well, right now you're acting like a child, and I'm glad I didn't come." He then blocked me.

"What the F*CK just happened?" I asked myself in the mirror before drinking more champagne."I'm cursed! How do things like this keep happening to me?" I threw myself on the bed and began to cry."I'm going to be alone forever." I sobbed until I fell asleep.

CHAPTER TWENTY-THREE

"Say My Name" ~ Destiny's Child

I didn't know the answers, so I decided to go to a psychic medium for some advice and support; we'd spoken before lockdown and everything he'd said had come true.

"Hello again, L.J. It's nice to see your face. Look at all that hair!" The psychic smiled at me across FaceTime.

"Thanks, full head of hair extensions. I love it." I tossed my hair around and giggled.

"So, I'm picking up a lot of things right away." He looked at me intensely."You've just come into a bit of money," he stated.

"Yes, I have." I didn't give much away.

"There's going to be more, but please don't tell anyone. When you get it, keep it to yourself."

"Is it related to my books?" I looked hopeful.

"Yes, but more than books—TV, a movie," he continued."Keep this one to yourself. Finances are going to really improve soon."

"Well, I couldn't be any more broke." I laughed, remembering my hardship. For years now, I'd not been able to afford to eat well or pay my bills, and I was tired of it.

"Now, your love life… it's complicated. You're in love."

"Yes, very much so!" My heart pounded.

"He's not the right man. It's not going to work out. It's a bad outcome, I'm afraid. You'll be very hurt. He's got a dark secret." He shook his head and paused.

"Are you sure? I'm certain he's the one." I shook my head in disbelief.

"He'll come back from time to time, to use and abuse. Nothing more will come of this. It's dark energy." He looked at me with sympathy.

"But, but…" I couldn't believe how devastating this made me feel.

"I see another man. His name is Jamie or James."

"Oh gosh, don't you remember—last time we spoke you said, 'the one' was called Jamie?" I looked at him in shock.

"Did I really? I don't remember any of our readings, I'm afraid. I'm in a trance… He's a boxer, retired, and around 36 years old." He continued like he was visualising him, and it freaked me out.

"A toy boy," I scoffed."I never go for younger men; they don't have enough life experience." I shook my head, pushing the thought away."And I've never had any connection with the boxing world. I don't like fighting."

"You meet in August, and you sleep together that night."

"We do? I will?" I couldn't imagine sleeping with anyone other than

Fox.

"It's not until the second time you sleep with him that he falls in love with you." He smiled and nodded to himself.

"Someone actually falls in love with me?" I stared in amazement.

"Madly, deeply, in love with you; like nothing you've ever experienced. Oh. Okay. I see." He talked to himself for a minute then paused again."He's also a bit of a writer; this is how you connect. You've a lot in common with your past, too. He's an old soul, he's been through a lot. He's really good with children. I see a lot of children around you both. Perhaps he starts to train them. You'll get involved with this, and it will lead to a children's book."

"A children's book? I wouldn't know where to start. I write erotica," I laughed playfully.

"You've written quite a few good books, but don't be surprised if they ask for another one. You're going to be popular."

"Oh, I hope so. I've not done very well—hardly sold any of them so far." I felt frustrated by all my hard work and no real results.

"Well, don't be surprised if there's a movie. There might actually be a few!"

"Jesus, really?" I sat up in shock.

"This sounds crazy even to me, but there's a director who goes by the name 'Zombie.'" He scratched his head.

"Never heard of anyone by that name." I looked at him confused.

"Yep, that's very clear, he has zombie in his name, or nick name. He has ties with the music world, which is something you'll also be connected with."

"I can't sing. I'm tone deaf."

"But you can rhyme and write music," he insisted. I opened and closed my mouth in shock. I'd written a song for Fox just a few weeks ago.

"Ha! Okay." He nodded again."The books are rude and funny. They're very good. They'll ask you to play a part in it." He seemed amused.

"This is unreal! All my dreams would come true."

"They do, they do," he reassured me."I see you in LA and London mostly, but Jamie will take you on holiday to Hawaii. You'll be walking on a hot beach. You must do as you're told and wear sandals or you'll hurt your feet. This is where he asks you to marry him."

"What the F*CK? I get married again?"

"Yes, and you settle down for good and write children's books. The books you write now make your life comfortable, and it's how Jamie knows."

"Knows what?"

"That there's a woman out there who will give him unconditional love. He's been very sad."

"But what about Fox?" I bit my lip and welled up.

"There's a fight, a big fight… between Jamie and Fox. He won't let go of you easily. By the time he knows what he's lost, it's too late for him."

"I don't want Fox to get hurt." I felt tears forming.

"He starts the fight. It's a bad situation, but it will pass." We both paused as I took the information in.

"You can't trust your family, and some of your friends talk about you behind your back. They say you're not going to make it. You mustn't listen to any negative vibrations. Push forward! Now, your health." He shook his head, then nodded, talking to himself again internally."Your joints, knees, and back—you need to go to see a doctor."

"I've already been, about six weeks ago, because my knees started to hurt." I looked at him in amazement.

"Your back will start next. You must look after yourself. Drinking needs to be reduced; you're dehydrated, and it's not helping this situation."

"Is there any chance you could have all this completely wrong? I mean, I love Fox; no one could compete. The career stuff is great, but I don't even have an agent after the last one sacked me."

"America is where things start. Trust the process. You deserve this. And please don't forget me when you're rich and famous!" We both beamed at each other, and I cried."That's our time up, L.J. It's been a pleasure doing your reading today. Oh, one last thing they are telling me before we go: when you're on the set, be prepared for lots of waxing." I burst out laughing through the tears and ended the call.

Fox and I are going to end forever? And who the f*ck is Jamie?

CHAPTER TWENTY-FOUR

"War Pigs" ~ Black Sabbath

On 24th February 2022, the Russians began their invasion of Ukraine. The news was devastating, and it shook the world to its core—the second devastating blow since Covid. The world seemed to have lost its mind, and it felt like it was taking me with it. We were just getting over a global pandemic and now a megalomaniac was out to take over the world. We would probably, I guessed, be in a Third World War by winter, or worse, nuked! Life seemed so hard without any other life pressures. It was a crazy time to be alive, like living in a bad movie.

Fox and I were at our darkest place. We hardly communicated. It was the worst it'd ever been. It felt like we were completely drifting apart, not only as lovers but as friends. Weeks had passed, and I'd found comfort once again with Mr Belfast; only ever over text, though, as his time was taken up with his children and work. I never came first, which seems the story of my life, but he was there when Fox wasn't.

Mr Belfast seemed to be my go-to when anything ever went wrong, but he wasn't Fox, so no matter what he said and did it wouldn't be good enough. I sent him a text to keep him in the loop with what was going on in my life as regularly as I could, but he found it hard to find the time to respond. Similar to Fancy Pants, he mostly ignored me, and it made me feel like I was going to disappear.

"Hey, I'm really upset. My brother's on his way to Kyiv; his wife's parents live there. I'm worried sick he'll not come back." I sent the text. He replied unusually fast and in capitals.

"Look, I know you mean well, but I have best mates who text me less than you! I don't have time to text all day," he snapped back.

"What?" I replied madly at him."So, I tell you I'm upset for good reason, and you think about too many f*cking text messages? There's a war breaking out, and my brother might get blown up. Where's your heart?" I was so mad I blocked him immediately and threw my phone down onto the table. I couldn't believe his cold response. How could he? All I could hear in my head was THIS IS NOT NORMAL!

We could never go for long without becoming highly emotional. Perhaps it was the distance and sexual frustration, or something else was going on in his life? I guessed I'd never know, but I was definitely not prioritising him in my life; I'd seen too many negative things about him. We did this—had spats at each other, then blocked and unblocked again. It had been going on for months, so I knew I'd hear from him again. I didn't know why I gave him so many chances; there was just something about the relationship that I couldn't quite let go of. Moments later, my phone pinged with a text, and I thought it must be him apologising from another number, because this was his usual response, but instead it was Fox. I rolled my eyes and just wanted a break from men and all their drama.

"L.J., we need to talk."

"What about?" I replied.

"Breaking up—for good this time." I gulped and went to the kitchen to pour a glass of wine.

"Fox, we break up every week." I sent an emoji with rolling eyes.

"I'm going through a lot of changes, and I need time to rediscover myself. The cancer has changed me completely. I'm not the man I used to be."

"Have you seen the counsellor again?" I asked.

"I see her every week. She knows about us now, and it's helped for me to talk to someone about us. She thinks we're toxic together."

"Fox, she's right—we are toxic! But all I've ever done is love you." I drank more wine."Does the counsellor actually know us? No, she knows a textbook. Is she a qualified NHS counsellor? I'm glad you're going, but…"

"L.J., the world's in a mess, I'm in a mess, and I can't be there for you right now." He seemed very down.

"Well, you don't need to be—let me be there for you." I started to feel desperate to hold him.

"I don't depend on people," he snapped.

"I'm not telling you to depend on me; I'm offering my support. We've been through cancer together. We've been through everything. What are you doing? Trying to destroy us? This is us—we fight, and we make up, right?" I felt so desperate for him to understand me.

"I'm not fighting with you. I'm telling you I can't give you what you want or need. I can't do this anymore."

"Why, why can't you? Have you met someone new, someone better than me?" I was insecure and worried about losing him.

"NO… I can't go into it now."

"Tell me, I deserve to know!" I demanded an answer.

"L.J., you're in love with me, and I'm not in love with you!" There were a few minutes before I was able to reply.

"You don't love me?" I started to shake.

"No, I don't love anyone." It was a cold calculated response.

"But our sex life?" My lip quivered.

"Yes, it was extraordinary, exceptional, and I love what we've had, but it's over." I began to cry.

"Look, the cancer might be back. I won't know for a week. I've noticed some changes." I froze in disbelief.

"What are your symptoms?" I felt winded.

"Just a few new things. I don't want to discuss it." I could see now why he was pushing me away again; he must have been in so much turmoil and scared.

"I'm not leaving your side, even if you push me away and tell me to stay out of it!"

"I need you to, L.J. I'll let you know my results, but I need you to exit my life. We're not together and we never have been, so just GO, okay? Leave me alone!"

"Really, you want me to go?" I was now a pathetic mess.

"YES. Please go away. I'm blocking you. Don't message me in any way." He was gone. I threw my wine glass across the room, and it hit the wall where it smashed into a million pieces—just like my heart.

I'll Never Love Again was playing on Alexa. I curled myself up in a ball and sobbed on the floor next to my laptop. It felt like my life was falling apart and that I'd never recover, that I was equally as sick as him—he'd broken me.

"I love you, stupid man," I screamed at the top of my voice, putting my face in my hands, crying inconsolably, and rocking like a baby; he'd tipped me over the edge.

The only way I ever dealt with my emotions was to write. Instead of sending a million emails to him begging him to reconsider, I'd take out my frustrations with my words and write about how I felt.

My Gmail was already open and, with eyes blurred from the tears, I started to read all my correspondence from him over the years: hundreds of emails, love letters, photos of places he'd been, hotel booking confirmations, and events we'd attended together for work. It was comforting to have something to read to confirm it was real, had happened, and that he used to want me.

I scrolled down and found one from an editor I'd been talking to throughout lockdown who lived in America and was extremely well known for his excellence. We'd met on Twitter, and he'd read through A Year of SINatra and liked it. I felt privileged to be talking to him, let alone sending him my new work. We'd been arranging for months for me to potentially visit him and go through the first draft of the third book. He just 'got' my work and was such a great teacher; I felt like the Karate Kid, and he was Mr Miyagi.

Hi, L.J.,

I'd be delighted to do the final edit with you, and the dates in June work for me. Here's a list of hotels that are near me. Let me know when your flights are booked, and I will set a schedule for the week.

It'll be a full five days of editing and rewriting—lots of hard work! Be prepared!

Oh, and it'll be 100 degrees and humid out here so bring the appropriate clothing; it's going to be a shock to you from the British weather.

Looking forward to seeing you then.

Best,
M

I stared at my laptop in amazement. "I'm really going to America!" I cried and smiled at the same time, putting my hands together in prayer. This was exactly what I needed. I couldn't believe my luck—it was a light in the darkness.

"F*ck, how the hell am I going to afford it?"

CHAPTER TWENTY-FIVE

"Bad Ass Motherf*cker" ~ Hardcore Troubadours

Instead of becoming my usual train wreck, I got angry and motivated. I wasn't going to cry over someone who didn't love me. I wasn't going to let him drag me into the seventh level of hell or to the bottom of a bottle of wine. I was going to pick myself up and do something to shift his negative energy from my life. Sure, he'd broken my heart and made me feel so unimportant I thought I was about to disappear. He'd taken away my confidence, self-respect, dignity, and pride, but he could never take away my writing—no one could.

SINatra was out and already sales were picking up; I'd had a few reviews on Goodreads and random fans followed me. So far, feedback was mostly positive, which was reassuring. Now, I was faced with the biggest challenge of my life—writing the back story of all of it, book three!

Each morning, I looked in the mirror while brushing my teeth and told myself to fight for me, and not to fall apart. I would shout at my reflection if I had any negative thoughts about my abilities, and repeat,"Get a hold of yourself and move forward; you've a book to write. Pick yourself up and dust yourself down!"

My soul and spirit fought so hard to rescue me back from the darkness I'd fallen into. The hardest thing was not reaching for a bottle of wine, because I knew it would make me lose my focus. It used to help me write, but now hindered it. I had to become teetotal and take out my addiction with my running shoes. Sometimes I'd run so hard my feet would blister. I forced myself forward and worked harder than I'd ever worked. What did I want to tell people? How did I want them to see me? What was I trying to get across?

I had no backup, family, or friends who would help fund my trip to Alabama; I was on my own. I took an extra job as a part-time hotel receptionist to pay for it, in addition to working as a recruitment consultant and a writer. I was also still single parenting two hormonal teenagers. I never stopped working, but nothing would get in the way of this trip.

I couldn't watch or listen to anything to do with love; re-living everything that'd happened to me and writing about it was enough. I hoped that if I talked about it enough, I would somehow become de-sensitised to it, like binge watching scary movies and not getting frightened any more. I played heavy dance music and rave because it took me away from my feelings, motivating and lifting me away from the pain.

Rejection was something I'd had to deal with all my life from childhood right through work and relationships. The only thing that never said"I don't love you" were my books. I made my own reality, and I was in love with my passion more than I'd ever been in love with anyone or anything else.

I wrote and wrote. If this book was going to be the end of the trilogy, people were going to know exactly who I was, why I was the person I'd become, and how I believed all my life experiences had come about, good and bad. I wanted people to see ME. I wasn't afraid or ashamed of anything I'd written. In fact, the more real I could be, the better. Why should I hold anything back? It was my life; it was true; it'd happened to me.

I took up kickboxing, swimming, dance, singing, and art. I even started a podcast. For months I did everything I could to distract myself or inspire me to write the book.

Most people kept me at a distance. People I'd known all my life disappeared. The same had happened with the first book, but the second book we'd been in a lockdown. I noticed how I changed and how people couldn't be around me when I was so focused—apart from a few. One of them who surprised me after our many fall outs was Mr Belfast. He'd become a leaning post, one I'd ignored for so long because of Fox and Fancy Pants.

I looked at my diary and started to read the contents of the past year. Closing my eyes, I relived the past as my fingers moved down the page. I made notes as I went along and tuned into my music playlist. I had a connection with music just as much as I did words. I started to pace around the room with my diary, instructing Alexa to find songs associated with key words from the journal."Alexa, find songs with 'f*cking.'"

She replied saying she didn't know that one, so I googled them on my phone instead.

"Alexa, play 'Smells Like Teen Spirit' by Nirvana." The request was accepted, and I thought about my past, when I was a child, and where my passion for writing had started. I was overwhelmed with emotions and found it easy to flood the pages with words. Typing fast, my fingers banged on the letters of the keyboard.

"Publisher" my phone announced on caller ID, and I answered, breaking my creativity.

"L.J., How are you? We've arranged an interview with a boxer, the punk kid for research; can you call him ASAP? He's happy to introduce you to fight talk. Don't miss out on this. No one else is available."

"Yeah sure, no problem. Shoot over his details, and I'll call him today," I said, typing my last sentence, then giving them my full attention."Any updates on book signings?" I gave a big sigh—no one seemed to want me in their stores, probably because of the content of the books. When was I ever going to get noticed? I felt frustrated at how slow a process it was.

"Nothing so far, L.J." The tone in her voice said it all.

"Okay, thanks. I'll call Jack today and send you across my notes."

"Looking forward to it, L.J. Good luck. Oh, and safe flight to Alabama!"

The boxer I was about to interview was young, enthusiastic, and a self-confessed punk called Jack. I'd driven to a pub in the middle of nowhere to do the interview over FaceTime, but when I arrived it was shut. So, I parked up and prayed for good coverage. I got my notepad and pen ready, but I was really nervous as I knew hardly anything about boxing and didn't want to come across as an idiot. I really hoped he could give me exactly what I was looking for: how to talk FIGHT—it was exactly what I needed right now.

I dialled his number and switched it to FaceTime, propping my phone on the dash as far away as possible. He answered and his face was there, smiling, and friendly at the other end."Hi, Jack, it's nice to meet you! Thank you for doing the interview. When I spoke to your trainer,

I explained that I'm looking for some fight talk to give my book a bit more attitude. I need some inspiration; I feel like I need to end it with some serious attitude. Is this something you can talk to me about? Your emotions in the ring are probably the same for so many wanting to get things off their chest."

"Yes, that's fine with me. I'm happy to help." He seemed at ease and a lovely guy, not anything like I'd expected.

"So, let me tell you my back story, then you'll be able to understand what I'm doing. I've been writing a real-life story over the past six years, from when I left my husband. I was married a long time, he cheated, and we never recovered from it, so I left. Then I went online dating, documented it, and wrote my first book, which I left on a cliff-hanger. Then I wrote another after meeting someone new. Now I'm on my third book, and I'm working with a top editor in America—flying out in June to do the final edit. We're hoping for a movie, but it's all pie in the sky right now; leaving it up to fate. The books are a little racy, but because it's a true story I think the public will love it. I'm tragically single, recovering from heartbreak, and I need some fight talk."

I took a deep breath."So, you still okay to do the interview?" He looked back at me with amazement at the overshare.

"Yes, absolutely. Where would you like me to start?"

"From the beginning, I guess. How did you get involved in boxing?" I started to take notes.

"Well, I wasn't bullied or anything like that. It wasn't for getting stronger or fighting back. I had a great childhood. I watched a boxing match—I'd never watched one before—and I was just hooked. I loved it, and I just knew it's what I was supposed to do!" Jack spoke gently and didn't look aggressive, more like Kurt Cobain than Mike Tyson. He had such a unique image. He was like a gentle warrior.

"As an amateur, I trained at 'Hooks,' and as a pro at 'State of Mind,' which I have tattooed on me. I love my tattoos. It's funny you should mention fate. I have 'Do you believe in fate?' tattooed on me too. I've had a lot of achievements. However, boxing comes with other things to overcome. You can't ever give in; you have to work toward your best performance all the time."

"What other hardships are there to overcome?" I was hooked on his story already. He sounded just like me, but with different challenges and a different talent.

"Ticket sales—you have to generate enough to actually have the fight. And opponents cancelling a fight at the last minute. Sometimes you have to put your own money into it." I looked at him surprised and had a flashback to my publishers asking me to pay thousands for the publication of my first two books, which nearly destroyed me financially, but I was so passionate in the end goal I just did it.

"It's also about standing out and being unique. In the ring, I wear half shorts, half pink skirts, nail varnish, and lipstick. I have an image to maintain, and people seem to really love it."

"No way—that's awesome! I love that you get in the ring looking like that." I beamed at him in amazement."I myself am unique, probably a bit too much for some people. But it's all about being your real authentic self, right?"

"Yes, and building the brand." He nodded in agreement.

"So, I've got the back story. Didn't you retire during the Covid pandemic for a bit, but are back on it now, stronger than ever?" I took notes, then the signal dropped, and I lost him."F*ck!" I grabbed the phone and tried to make it work again."Work, you stupid f*cking thing!" I redialled but couldn't connect so just called him and put it on speaker.

"Sorry, Jack, I'm in the middle of nowhere; we'll have to do it this way if that's okay? So, where were we? Can I ask about your emotions leading up to a fight and when you're in the ring?"

"Okay, so, I guess a lot of other boxers talk about getting psyched up before the match, but I don't really. I have a laugh with my coach and don't really think about it. Then I get in the ring, and I can hear all the sound and cheering around me, but I just focus on my opponent, and I don't hear the sound anymore; it's just me and him in the ring, fighting, until I win."

My mind drifted as he was talking, and suddenly I imagined myself there, only it wasn't Jack in the ring; it was me. I stood in the dark with a spotlight on me. I was dressed in black silk shorts and a matching crop top with a towel around my neck, wearing red boxing gloves.

"Okay, subconscious, what's going on now?" I shouted into the darkness.

"Hello, L.J.," a voice came from one dark corner of the ring, then another, and another. I recognised them all.

"Dad?" I'd always called him this growing up, even though he wasn't my real father.

"Hello, L.J. Gosh you've grown up." He came out of the darkness and stared at me emotionless.

"Well, I haven't seen you for 27 years," I hissed at him. I hated this man; every part of my body tensed and became defensive.

"Looks like we have company. Did you invite your friends? I thought you never had any," he said darkly.

"Hello, L.J.," a voice walked out from the shadow; it was Fancy Pants, dressed in black silk shorts to match me with 'Fancy' written in gold down one side. He playfully started to pretend to box around me.

"Fancy Pants, you couldn't frighten a worm." I looked directly at his penis, then back to his eyes. I laughed at him, sticking out my tongue.

"Last surprise!" Fox's voice came from another side of the ring. He was dressed in a smart suit with no gloves on.

"Fox, go away. I can't fight you. I won't hurt you." I turned my back and put my hand up to him, pushing him away.

"Who says I'm here to fight you?" A pair of gloves were thrown to him, and he walked over to my stepdad, slowly put them on, then punched his hands together, right in his face.

"So, we're doing this together?" I questioned his actions.

"I'm here to support you," he whispered gently into my ear."Let's f*ck them up!"

I clapped my gloves."Music, play Bad Motherf*cker, MGK, Kid Rock; it's Jack's favourite."

"Who's Jack?" Fancy Pants looked confused.

"He's a badass motherf*cker who taught me how to kick your ass." I raised my eyebrows at him."So, who's first?" I put my mouth shield in and grinned; it was not sexy. Then I put my fists in the air.

They turned to each other, and both pointed to the other, saying,"Him." My stepdad put one foot forward and laughed.

"You won't be laughing in a minute!" We circled each other, not breaking eye contact.

"You're useless. Always have been. You'll never come to anything. Your books are a joke." He gritted his teeth and looked at me with anger in his eyes. Every part of my being filled with hate and disgust. I launched at him with the first punch. The rush filled my veins; I felt so powerful.

"I'll keep going until you fall, fat old man." I launched another punch into his stomach, then a left uppercut. Blood spurted out of his mouth."Come on, f*cking hit me—you're used to hitting women, right? You're a pathetic piece of sh*t! Get up and fight!" He launched a punch and it missed."Jack, what now? Where do I hit him?"

"Right hook and duck out of his way." I smashed my fist into his body and moved away quickly. It felt good.

"Not so nice when someone does it to you, is it, DAD!" I inhaled through my nose and began bouncing around him, filled with adrenaline.

"Jab. Now, L.J., straight down the middle. Hit him harder." Jack instructed me further. I hit him hard again, making aggressive sounds. Sweat started to drip off me.

Fancy Pants joined the ring."Let's take her down," my stepdad summoned to him.

"That's not the rules! One at a time," I argued.

"It's okay, L.J., I know you won't hit me—you worship me, you always have." Fancy Pants looked at me with amusement.

"Oh really? I won't? Why do you think you're here today? Because you pissed me off, that's why!"

"What are you going to do, write another book about me? Oh my, I'm so scared." He burst into laughter and looked at my stepdad to fist bump.

"Left hook to the chin, L.J." Jack knew all the moves, and Fancy Pants flew across the ring, knocked out.

"Not so fancy now, are you? Should have treated me like a lady and not used me as your puppet." Glaring at him, I smacked my boxing gloves together and got ready to finish what I'd started. A person in the audience waved and caught my attention; it was Mr Belfast.

"This is a great show! Do you know how hot you look?" He stuffed popcorn into his mouth and with his other hand, adjusted his pants awkwardly."This is the L.J. we want!"

"Come on, old man, give it your best," I taunted. He took a few swings and hit me in the stomach, bringing me to my knees.

"Get up, L.J." Jack's voice came from the distance in desperation as I was hit around the head again and again. My ears rang, and blood came out of my nose. It was my childhood all over again; he was winning, and I was helpless and weak."GET UP! FIGHT!" The voice spoke to me almost in slow motion as I staggered to my feet, my outfit and body covered in blood. I wiped my face with my glove and launched into him with a 90-degree hook."Uppercut, L.J., as many times as you can!" Jack's voice was louder and stronger.

"You'll never make it. I told you this when you were little, every day." My stepdad tried to hit me with words, not able to use his fists.

"You're not going to be the reason I fail any more. I've been fighting you ALL MY LIFE." I screamed aggressively, trying to get out of a head lock, but he had hold of me too tightly.

"You're useless. You're ugly. You're thick. You're a pointless human, and always will be," he continued as I hit him as hard as I could, struggling to get out of his grip."You couldn't even keep a husband." He gritted his teeth as he lifted his right arm, ready to punch me in the face. I broke free and ducked.

"I f*cking left him," I screamed and threw a punch to his face, making him fall to the floor. Mr Belfast whistled and clapped in the background.

"Go on, L.J., let it all out!" He continued to stuff his face with popcorn, clapping his hands together in applause and blowing kisses!"Bravo!"

"You're nothing but a cheap slag." He slowly got to his feet, ready to fight again.

"That's IT," Fox's voice came from behind me."L.J., stand back. You've proved your point." And with one punch from Fox, my stepdad was knocked to the floor."She's not a slag, and she's won. Now leave, get away from her and leave her alone or you'll have me to f*cking deal with." He pointed to the exit. We watched him pull himself up and start to drag himself away.

"Aww, bye bye, Daddy, I'll really miss you. Not." I took off my glove and gave him the finger as he took one last defeated look at me. I watched him walk into the darkness and felt like my life's chains were removed. I'd stood up to my biggest fear. My emotions decreased, and I found freedom from my anxiety, like a bird set free into the sky. It was a pivotal, peaceful moment. I turned to Fox, took off our gloves, and held his hands in mine, then looked around."Where's Fancy Pants?" I couldn't see him.

"He had a date, had to dash," Fox said, laughing loudly, and it echoed around the room.

"I feel a bit bad; I hope I didn't hurt him too much. I don't think he's that much of a bad person really." I shrugged."He's just a bit of a dick."

"Some fight you put up there, young lady." He kissed me on my forehead and pulled me close. I pulled away, still slightly bruised from him dumping me. I was confused.

"Well, thank goodness for Jack!" I backed away, but all I wanted to do was move close to him.

"Yeah, he's awesome, a superstar waiting to happen." He pushed my hair back and kissed my lips, still covered in blood.

"Thank you for sticking up for me and having my back." I looked into his eyes lovingly but confused by him.

"I know you needed to beat the crap out of him. I've known for years, but I had to throw the last punch. Sorry if I stole your thunder." I shook my head as it wasn't a problem.

"So, what's next, Fox?"

"You move on from me. I'm holding you back. Go to America, and please try not to punch anyone if they piss you off—they'll chuck you out!" he teased. He walked over to the corner of the ring and picked up my brown leather briefcase that I took everywhere and placed it over my shoulder.

"Go, get out of here! Finish the third book, L.J. Show everyone what you're made of, show the world the real you, and don't care about what other people think. Never stop fighting. You just got over your past; now get over me!"

CHAPTER TWENTY-SIX

"Don't Know Much" ~ Aaron Neville and Linda Ronstadt

Fox and I remained separated, and I spent the next few weeks finishing the book and taking time out from everything to just focus. A few days before I was due to fly out to America, Mr Belfast contacted me to let me know that he was coming to Yorkshire and asked to meet me for a drink. I wasn't sure it was a good idea, but it felt like we had unfinished business and was another part of my past that I needed to try to understand.

I couldn't believe the day we were to meet again was finally here; he'd confirmed that he'd arrived in Yorkshire and what time he would be available. My gut gave me such mixed messages: do I go, or do I stay home? I was desperate to find out if the connection was still there between us, but something deep inside told me not to go. Maybe it was the fact that he'd stood me up before, and I was worried I'd get there, and he wouldn't be reachable. I was curious but not really excited, which made me worry that the date wasn't going to go well.

Of all the places he could pick, not knowing Yorkshire well, he'd found a manor house close to where I used to live with my ex-husband. Driving there brought back so many memories, ones I cared to forget. It gave me chills even on a warm summer's day. I had so much to do before my flight to America; everything was spinning around in my head, and I couldn't fully relax or appreciate what was about to happen.

I stopped at a petrol station nearby to pick up some chewing gum.

Standing in the queue was a tall, dashing man, his hair jet black, slightly greying at the sides. I could only see the back of him, but he looked familiar to me. He went to the till to pay and spoke in his thick Yorkshire accent,"Pump two." I knew immediately that it was Fancy Pants. Years had gone by since we were in the same room, and I felt my heart start to pound and ring in my ears; all the old feelings rushed back to me. I darted out of the queue and, like a naughty child, terrified he might see me, hid in one of the aisles.

Oh my God, I still completely adore him, I thought in surprise. Not knowing what to do with what'd just happened to me, I re-joined the queue and paid, taking my time as I watched him pull away in a Porsche with a stunning blonde in the passenger seat. My mind raced as I followed the satnav to the hotel where Mr Belfast was staying. What was that? Why did that have to happen at this precise time? What did it even mean? And why did I still have such an intense feeling for him?

I arrived in the car park and texted to see if he was ready to meet. A few minutes later, he replied, and asked me to meet him in ten minutes. Thank God I wasn't going to get stood up again!

"F*ck, it's really happening!" I said to myself in the mirror of my car and reapplied my red lipstick. I'd gone for a casual look: tight black jumper dress, heels, and a light blue denim jacket. I'd dyed my hair the day before, which accentuated my big blue eyes, and had done a great job with my make-up. I stepped out of my car and looked all around; the manor house was vast and beautiful—it took my breath away. It had so much history.

Another text came:"It's room 203. I'll meet you outside the room." I took a deep breath and blew my hair away from my face.

I was surprised we weren't meeting at the bar, but replied,"Okay, see you there. X," then walked through reception to the elevator and pressed the button for the second floor. 'Ping'—the doors opened, and I walked out, expecting him to be there or nearby, but he wasn't. I walked down the corridor to find the room, stopping to lean against the wall for a moment and check my phone. The elevator pinged again, and I stood up straight, put my phone in my pocket, and watched the tall dark-haired man I'd met four years earlier approach me, looking right into my eyes. My body felt frozen to the spot.

"Look at you. What's it been—four years? I'm sorry I'm in shorts and t-shirt," he apologised as he clearly saw I'd made an effort. He kissed me on my lips and gave me a hug. We stood looking at each other for a few moments, smiling like teenagers, then he got his key card out and tried to open the door to his room. It didn't work. He tried again, looking at the card and then the door."Oh, God, I've got the wrong room here," he apologised nervously,"We're in 204." He shook his head and laughed, walking to the next room.

"Have you been drinking?" I made a joke out of the situation, trying to put him at ease.

"Just had a few pints at the bar." He was clearly nervous. Entering, I put my bag down on the table and we stood in front of each other. He put his hands on my waist and leaned in to kiss me. He tasted of beer and smelt of aftershave. When I first met him, our kiss was like a bolt of lightning—I'd felt the current go through my body, we were charged. This time, something had changed; I didn't feel the WOW factor. Was this because I was sober or because of Fox, or because I'd just encountered Fancy Pants.

The kiss didn't last long, and he stood back and looked at me again." "You look great! I love your ass in that dress!" He tried to compliment me. His physique had changed, but his beautiful deep blue eyes were the same.

"I brought some vodka and orange." I pointed to the bag I'd put down. "You said we could sit, get drunk, and talk?" I looked for glasses.

"I want to see your tattoo first." He threw me onto the bed, and I yelped. He pushed my dress up and pulled my panties down slowly, running his fingers over the tattoo. Then, looking right into my eyes, he went down on me. I loved the effort and the fun, but it still felt nothing like it had before—this was a bad sign. If we were going to have sex tonight this was not a good start. I faked an orgasm to make him feel manly, then said I needed a drink to relax. I hadn't faked it in years, so this felt strange; what was wrong with me?

"What vodka did you get?" He examined the bottle. "Oh God, I'm going to need to get some mixers. This isn't the stuff I'd usually drink." I wasn't a vodka drinker, so didn't really know what was good or bad. "I'm going to nip down to the bar and get some mixers." He grabbed his card, gave me another quick kiss, and left the room in a hurry. When he'd gone, I looked around for inspiration, got the vodka, and poured myself a large glass with orange, then downed it. I repeated this a few times while stripping off all my clothes and scattering them around the room.

"What can I do that's fun?" I looked around and saw the window was open and it had long curtains that dropped to the floor. "That's it, hide and seek!" I quickly hid behind the curtain and waited for him to return. The door unlocked and he walked in; I stood still and quiet behind the curtain, trying not to giggle.

"L.J., where're you at?" his Irish accent was so much sexier after a few shots of vodka."Come out, come out, wherever you are." He giggled, then pulled back the curtain.

"BOO!" I shouted, then fell into fits of laughter.

"Oh, look at that body." He scanned me."I like that." He pointed to my pussy, lifting me up onto the windowsill and fully opening the curtains.

"What're you doing?" I looked shocked, my bare bottom exposed and hanging out of the window.

"I'm going to f*ck you." He dropped his shorts and kissed me hard so I couldn't object as he entered me slowly. I'd forgotten how large his penis was and it shocked me, taking my breath away just as much as it'd done the first time.

"Stop! We shouldn't. People can see," I tried to get him to pull me down and onto the bed, but he f*cked me harder and faster. I heard drunk people below laughing, and he looked right into my eyes, and grinned wickedly—he was loving this.

"I told you you'd like to be watched," he said devilishly, then pulled out, carried me over to the bed, and placed me down. He kissed the tattoo at the top of my pussy, then all over my body like he was saying hello to it again.

"I've put a bit of weight on since lockdown, I've not got the supermodel body I once had." I saw him look over every inch of me, taking in everything.

"The only things that look bigger to me are your tits." He squeezed them and jiggled them around.

"I know, right? I used to have Keira Knightley tits. Apparently, it's called a middle-aged rack. I'm getting old! At least they're still pert, I guess," I giggled.

He got up, showing me his stomach."No six pack anymore—covid weight. We've all put some on, L.J." I covered my mouth with one hand and pulled him back down to the bed, giggling.

"You're still sexy as f*ck," I said, kissing his lips softly. We locked eyes and he crawled over me, parting my legs, and entered me again. I couldn't think, I couldn't speak, and I couldn't breathe, as he literally worshiped me, f*cking me slowly and deeply, not taking his eyes off me. He kissed me passionately on my neck, my face, and lips, and we were both building together, our bodies in perfect tune until he put his hand around my neck. I pulled it away. I'd had this done once before, and I didn't like it. He apologised.

"L.J., I'm going to cum." He pulled out and came all over my pussy."F*ck me, that was a hard cum." He flopped onto the bed to the side of me."Now," he said, out of breath,"You wanted to talk?" He turned to me and kissed me again, smiling and panting into my mouth.

"I think I better clean up first." My eyes pointed to the mess he had made all over me."You do know I've been sterilised, right? I can't get pregnant."

"I know, but you can never be too careful." He got up and walked over to the bottle of vodka while I visited the bathroom to clean myself up. When I returned, he had two glasses on the bed with the vodka and mixers, and he'd placed a towel over his penis.

"What are you covering up for?" I took the towel off and kissed his penis.

"I'm shy," he giggled and started pouring us both a drink. He had the most amazing laugh; it made me constantly smile.

"So, the beard is new." I pulled my fingers through his thick bushy beard and wrinkled my nose.

"I know, I love it. It's staying." He sipped his vodka, still looking at me.

"To finally meeting after four years." I raised a toast.

"I can't believe we haven't got together in so long." His face looked astonished.

"Well, take two years away for lockdowns and the end of the world," I shook my head in disbelief at what we'd all gone through and how surreal it still was."We should've got our acts together, but both of us have been a bit busy." I drank my vodka back and reached for the bottle.

"God, you can drink, Lady." He chuckled.

"Doesn't this feel weird to you?" I shrugged.

"What feels weird?" He looked concerned.

"That it's like we've never really been apart? I feel so comfortable in your company, and I've only met you once before."

"No, it's only weird when you get weird." He laughed loudly and fell into thought."You're a crazy bitch sometimes. You got a tattoo of my name after meeting me once, and you said you love me." He nudged me playfully.

"I do love you. I mean, I care about you a lot, you know this already. The tattoo was so I'd never forget you, a permanent reminder of a perfect night. It was supposed to be romantic and sexy." He fell silent.

I laid myself down on the bed on my front and he sat up next to the headboard."So, tell me about you; you never talk on text. You said you're better in person, and I think you're right!"

"I told you; I hate texting. It's so impersonal, and things get distorted."

"I like texting a bit too much."

"I like peace and quiet too. You're a bit full on with messages." His eyes were serious.

"I know, you told me like a million times. I get it, men don't like being chased." I threw another drink down and reached for the bottle.

"So, you've had so much going on, another child since we last met? What happened? How come you split up with her?"

"I wasn't even with her when she got pregnant, but I love him. He's the boss." He smiled widely, and I could tell he was a great dad.

"So, you tried to make it work, but it didn't?" I continued to question, as in the back of my mind I'd always been worried he was with someone and that was why he was never available to text or talk.

"She was too controlling. She's with someone else now, and he's a nice guy. I had him checked out. I'm happy enough for her." He seemed genuine, but it surprised me that he hadn't been in a serious relationship with her or anyone else.

"So, why're you still single? You're so attractive!" I blurted out without thinking.

"You've played on my mind for a few years," he said bashfully.

"You stalked me through my publisher, you psycho," I said, teasing him.

"You never texted me after we slept together." He was more serious now.

"I called you, once." I felt terrible knowing that Fox had been the reason why.

"Then you said you weren't interested in me." He searched me for an answer…"I live in Belfast, and you live in Yorkshire," he continued."I guess it could never work." My heart sank when he said the words, though I was unsure why.

"No, you're right—we can't ever be together. It just won't work." I nodded, and he agreed."I mean, we can't even text without getting into a fight." I tried to wrap my head around it.

"Long distance relationships rarely work. We should just f*ck each other whenever we can get the opportunity. We're pretty good at it." He tried to lighten the mood.

"Maybe. Let's see." I looked at him with sad eyes, and he leaned over to kiss me and pull me on top of him, letting me feel he was hard."AGAIN?" I looked shocked; I still had my glass in my hand. He took it off me and pushed himself inside me. Being on top, his size was even more apparent. We slowly picked up rhythm, and it was like time had literally stopped; I was completely lost in the moment.

He flipped me onto my back and pulled me down the bed."I only ever do this with you; I know you like it." He looked deep in concentration.

"Do what?" I smiled innocently at him, not knowing where he was going with this.

"THIS.". He sucked my breast and kissed my stomach, he kissed my entire body, squeezing my hand as my moaning became louder and louder. He picked up speed and went deeper and harder. No one had ever been this intense with me, he never took his eyes away from me, he was making love to me.

He didn't tell me he was going to cum; he just gave out a sound I'd never heard anyone make before, like a beast that'd just caught its prey. He fell apart and laid helpless on the bed for what seemed forever. I played with his chest hair and said nothing, in complete amazement at how good the sex had just been, yet I still hadn't had an orgasm. What the f*ck was going on? I always came with Fox.

"Come on, let's cuddle under the sheets and talk some more." He pulled me close to him and kissed my forehead.

My body made a sex sound caused by too much air from f*cking."Oh my God." I looked at him in shock, completely embarrassed."I'm sorry. Air must come out somehow, I guess," I continued, looking terrified, staring into his eyes, not knowing what to do; this had never happened to me before.

"It's fine. Look, I'll do one too, to make you feel better." He let out a little fart.

"You're kidding me. You did not just make yourself fart?" I laughed hysterically.

"It made you feel better, didn't it?" He got closer to my face and kissed me all over it, tickling me with his beard.

"You Irish nutter." I kissed him hard, and he was back inside me. I couldn't believe how much energy he had and how horny he was. This time, the orgasms came quick and strong, perhaps because we'd relaxed, and partly because we were a bit drunk, but mainly because I utterly adored him and felt safe. We came at the same time, and I screamed so loud he put his hand over my mouth to make me be quiet. He pulled me toward him, and we wrapped ourselves around each other. Thank God I'd finally had an orgasm.

"So, what's happening with the books and America?" he said, rubbing his eyes.

"Well, I fly out on Monday and meet the editor on my birthday the next day, go through the book and what needs changing, then I have a lot of work to do re-writing it, I guess." My mind filled with things I still had left to do.

"It's amazing, I'm really pleased for you. Just make sure you get the deal you deserve. Don't let anyone take advantage of you." He was serious now; he always was when it came to the subject of work.

"It's crazy to think that the last time we slept together, A Year of Tiramisu was only just out." I stared into his eyes."So, what now?" I asked, starting to fall asleep, but not wanting to miss out on anything.

"We go to sleep," he replied, totally spent.

"And then what?" I said, wearily.

"We will f*ck again in the morning." He pulled me toward his hairy chest, and I smelled our sex and his aftershave.

"And then what?" I started to be silly, and he smacked me with a pillow.

"Go to sleep, L.J." He kissed me and held his lips there to keep mine shut. He clearly didn't want to talk more.

I closed my eyes and without thinking about the words coming out of my mouth, I said,"Goodnight my naughty leprechaun, thank you for keeping your promise to see me again."

Back to the New York Times reporter.

"Oh my god, I love this; so, your love at first sight encounter was real; you guys still had this massive connection; he's got to be the one." He was beaming with hope that the situation was starting to get brighter for me.

"Maybe, who knows." I knew it wasn't the last time we'd communicate. We had some sort of invisible string connection that couldn't be broken.

"After that night, things started to get a little crazy with my career…" I poured a glass of water and continued to tell my story.

CHAPTER TWENTY-SEVEN

"Tennessee Whiskey" ~ Chris Stapleton

The night before my flight to America, sleep eluded me. The thought of an 8-hour journey to a place reputed for its high crime rate gnawed at my nerves, leaving me feeling alone and vulnerable. Tossing and turning, I reached for my phone, hoping for a distraction. To my surprise, a Facebook notification blinked at me. I squinted at the screen and saw a message from none other than Fancy Pants.

Startled, I bolted upright in bed. Even after all these years, he had an uncanny ability to command my attention instantly. My mind whirled as I fumbled to put on my glasses and read the message.

"I just read your message… a year late. How are you?" It was a reply to a message I had sent long ago, checking in on him without expecting any response.

"I'm on an early flight to America tomorrow," I typed back, adding a kiss emoji for good measure.

"You're really going for it, aren't you?" he replied.

"I told you; I always do what I set out to achieve," I responded, a smile tugging at my lips as I stared at the phone.

"I think I saw you at the petrol station a few days ago. I hid." My cheeks flushed with embarrassment at the memory.

"Why did you hide?" he sent a blushing emoji that made me chuckle.

"I've put on a little weight, and you were with some stunning blonde bombshell. I couldn't compete." I was glued to my phone, the adrenaline of hearing from him as intense as when we first started talking years ago.

"Are you still single? I hope you've stopped hanging around with FOX. He's clearly using you," he queried, catching me off guard.

"I seem to remember a certain someone doing the exact same thing to me," I replied, biting my lip, anticipating his witty retort.

"I'm in a relationship with myself and my career right now," I said confidently, though inwardly I felt a pang of sadness.

"So, he dumped you," he stated bluntly.

"Cheeky! Fox is not in a good place. You've missed out on a lot of my life over the past year. So much has happened!"

"Yeah, me too. I've just become single again, but don't want to talk about it it's been a difficult time.

"Take time out to heal," I added, more serious now.

"Did you actually really love me?" he texted in capitals, making my eyes widen. I started typing and stopped, taking a long time to find the right words. He began typing too but didn't send anything, both of us caught in a whirlwind of emotions.

"With all my heart and soul," I sent the message, unsure if my honesty would scare him away but feeling it was time to be truthful.

"That book you wrote, A Year of Tiramisu, you basically slagged me off, called me a narcissist. How can you do that and love me?"

"I was all consumed by you. I was confused; it was bittersweet. But you can't deny I tried to convey how crazy I was about you," I explained."I wrote that book to get you back."

"Well, it did the opposite, L J. It pushed me away from you."

"You said you'd never read the book?" I asked, puzzled by the sudden outpouring of emotions.

"Do you still love me, L J?" He seemed to seek some sort of clarification.

"You were my first love," I confessed."It was just very confusing for me."

"You were obsessed with me," he continued.

"I guess love can make you do stupid things," I admitted, falling back onto my bed, feeling the familiar flutter in my chest that always accompanied our conversations.

"But we had an agreement right from the start," he reminded me.

"Yes, and when I told you I had fallen in love, you should have called it off completely. But you didn't; you let me see you over and over again." My mind was a jumble of memories of us together.

"You lit me up. I felt like I was flying when I was with you. It was a euphoria I'd never experienced before. I wanted the dopamine hit from us," I confessed, surprised by my own honesty.

"We did have a lot of fun," he sent another blushing emoji.

"Are you drunk, Fancy Pants?" I sent a voice recording, teasing him.

"Not drunk enough. I'm running out. I might have to nip to the shops and get some more," he replied.

"Oh, we are feeling sorry for ourselves," I sent another voice note, my tone playful.

"I'm not a bad guy, you know. I have a good job. I look after my own home, pay my own bills. I have my shit together."

"I never said you didn't. I just think you struggle with holding a relationship down. Like I said, you need time out or at least some therapy."

"I don't need therapy," he texted in capitals, making me roll my eyes.

"Oh yes, that's right, you have me for every breakup disaster and depressive episode," I said sarcastically, then quickly softened my tone."I'm sorry. We're friends. I will always try my best to be there for you. I have a good heart too." I added a love heart emoji to my message.

"You're being a good friend tonight. Usually, you're a pain in the arse," he sent a kiss and a wink emoji.

"Here, listen to this song. Currently my favorite," he sent me a link to Tennessee Whiskey by Chris Stapleton. I blushed; he had never shared music with me before. This was a new side to him.

"What's your favorite love song?" he quizzed.

"Endless Love by Diana Ross and Lionel Richie," I replied without hesitation. I must have played it a million times in my life.

"We're both a pair of big softies. Why have we never communicated like this before?" I felt my heart swell with a mixture of nostalgia and longing.

"Because we hadn't grown up," he said boldly, and he was right.

"Sex is great, but love, sex, and companionship are all I crave now," I admitted, not seeing the point in holding back my thoughts as we spilled out our emotions.

"Wrong place, wrong time, huh? We met at the wrong time. Why did you not want to be with me anyway?" I sought some form of closure.

"You were a train wreck after your divorce. I didn't know what to do with you. Then there was the incident with my brother."

"That wasn't my fault. He came on to me. It says more about him than me, and besides, I never even met him." I felt anger simmer at the memory.

"Our situation is so complex, it's been really hard to deal with this over the years, we've been lovers, friends, enemies, friends again, don't you think it's time we closed the door?" I was hopeful he would say yes.

"We're friends, and I appreciate you being there for me tonight. I'm sorry I hurt you, but you hurt me too. All water under the bridge now. He surprised me by his comment.

"Tell you what, if we are both still single by the time, we are 90, I'll marry you", he teased.

"I'm sorry I hurt you". I text with a kiss.

"I'm sorry I hurt you too". He replied with two kisses, I was getting special attention, he was a sweet man after all.

I best let you get some sleep; you have a long flight tomorrow, good luck in life L J ." And just like that, Fancy Pants and I had made our peace and had complete closure, never to speak again.

CHAPTER TWENTY-EIGHT
BIRMINGHAM, ALABAMA, USA

"Born to be Wild" ~ Steppenwolf

After my breakup with Fox, my 2nd night of passion with Mr Belfast, and the conversation with Fancy Pants, it was safe to say I was still no closer to being 'Mrs Whoever' to any of them. In fact, I felt very single, and for the first time, I was really on my own. Not one of them wanted anything serious with me, but I reckoned all three would happily have sex with me if I clicked my fingers. I felt like all three of them had played an essential Lesson in my story. But everything felt like it was changing, ending or shifting, and moving on from my past, like I'd been tying up loose ends without realising I was doing it.

What was important now was getting to America. I'd taken a part-time job for minimum wage in a local hotel, checking guests in, cleaning up drunk people's vomit, and taking room service to executive suites where people shagged each other's minds out. I was still working in recruitment as well and trying to finish the book, so it was ready. I'd worked 15 hours a day for eight weeks while looking after two children. I was utterly exhausted.

I'd been warned that I was going to stay in the poorest and roughest part of Alabama, and on arrival, the hotel staff told me not to go outside at night by myself. The room didn't have a phone, the clock on the wall had stopped working, the bathroom had a leak from the ceiling, the toilet didn't flush very well, and only a few lights worked, but when they did, they flickered. The only saving grace was the air conditioning, as it was humid and 100 degrees. I'd never known heat like it. It'd hit me like a wall as soon as I got off the plane.

The first evening, I heard gunshots, so I slept in the bathroom with the door locked. I woke up the next morning and it was my birthday. I looked in the mirror and sang to myself, ecstatic that I was about to meet an absolute legend."Happy birthday to me, happy birthday to me, you're about to meet a fantastic editor and writer, happy birthday to me!"

I showered, then hurried around my room finding something executive but not too heavy to wear in the heat, applied my make-up, and did my hair the best I could; the humidity had made it wild and out of control. My phone buzzed and I went to read the message. It was Fox:"Happy Birthday, and good luck today." My heart squeezed that he'd thought of me, and that he'd worked out the time difference.

I locked the hotel door, rode in the elevator, walked through the hotel lobby, and arrived at the car park on time to wait exactly where I said I would. I saw a man in his late 60s walking toward me. Delighted, I smiled, and jumped up and down on the spot with joy.

"You must be the lovely L.J. Brown." He smiled widely and reached out to shake my hand, but instead I hugged him.

"You've no idea how much this means to me. Thank you so much for taking time out to see me." I couldn't believe I was in the presence of one of the best editors in the world.

"You're the one who's flown halfway across the world to meet me—the pleasure's all mine. Happy birthday!" he said, escorting me to his car."We're going to a diner to talk this manuscript over. We need it to be your very best work!" We talked in the car and got on like a house on fire. I'd never met another writer before, and it was amazing to have so much in common with someone. He thought like I did, and I no longer felt like a crazy person on the planet with billions of people who just didn't understand me.

After a short drive, we arrived at a traditional diner, a bit like I'd seen in the films; it had amazing atmosphere and the food smelt delicious. We sat down and both put the manuscript on the table, each covered in notes."So, what do you think of Alabama so far?" He got his pen out and peered down his glasses at me.

"It's very hot, my hotel is awful, and if I'm honest, I'm a little bit scared." I whispered so the locals didn't hear me."People are comparing me to Mary Poppins. It's quite amusing," I laughed and pulled out a notepad from my bag.

"I told you the hotel was in a bad area." He shook his head."You should've listened to me!" I blushed and looked at him for his instructions."So, I read through the manuscript, the story is good, it's strong. It has everything a reader would love to read about, but… it's not got a strong enough first and last chapter, and I can't work out the middle. Every good story, especially when we're thinking of making a movie, has to have a beginning, a middle, and an end. Where do you think the middle chapter is of the book?"

I flicked through the pages and couldn't work it out. I felt quite out of my depth for not having this knowledge already."Oh God, you're right." My mind was racing.

"The first chapter hooks people in, BANG, this book's going to be good, then the middle should be WOW, this book's getting even better, I must read on, and the last chapter needs to leave them begging for more. If it doesn't have those three fundamental chapters, the story doesn't glue together, it's just a series of scenes." I nodded and wrote down notes on what he'd just said.

"I'm going to say a few things you're not going to like, but it's how you use that information that'll count. Think like you're writing a movie; how would you want your readers to visualise it? Now, go to chapter one." I flicked through the dedications and the preface and got to chapter one."Read the first four paragraphs. You're rambling. I've already fallen asleep in my burger. Take it all out, the description and the build-up to the event, start at the event. He hit you with the pie and you get the hell out of there! The reader wants to get a sense of feeling what you're going through. Get to the point."

He was so strong with his wording and direction; I was overwhelmed by his way of looking at things and how his imagination worked."Lots of authors ramble for word count and over describe. You don't need to do that; it bores the reader. Just get to the point and tell the story. Make them engage with you from the first chapter. They'll want to know more about this mysterious creature I have in front of me." He gave me a cheeky smile of reassurance.

"The preface, rewrite it. It's not strong enough. Your alter ego's a badass but you're not showing the readers just how bad you are. It doesn't do you justice." I wrote on my pad, 'badass bitch.'"Now, the ending you've written is not the right end. The boxing match is good but it's not it; you've more chapters to write. This is not the full story. You've slept with the Belfast guy, talked to Fancy Pants, and fallen out with Fox all before flying over here, plus this trip—add them in. Honestly, I feel like your agony aunt as well as mentor with the amount of break ups and get back togethers with these three men." He was now amused.

"You also need a higher word count. We're on 60,000 and you need to be 90,000 plus. It won't be taken seriously if it's any less." My eyebrows raised at the amount of work he was setting me. I was still stressing over the fact my book didn't have a 'middle'—it was like having a hole in the story.

"Also, in my opinion, people like to see you've worked through something and got an end result, or solution, so they can learn from you. There isn't one, not that I can noticeably pick up on. And try to end it with some sort of clarification as to what you have or are about to achieve." He scrolled through the pages.

"L.J., if you want this to be a movie, you have to do the work. You have raw talent, there is no denying that, so make every word count."

"What do you think of my new title, Round One? I circled the same with my pen on the page.

"It's better than Madly in Love, but I'm still unsure. What do you have visualised for a front cover?" He started to make notes.

"I have this amazing image in my head. I tried to draw it but couldn't, so I've given it to an artist to do."

"Okay, what does it comprise?" He looked at me with interest.

"Imagine this: me, right in the middle, wearing black stockings and suspenders with red heels, a red boxing glove on one hand and a glass of wine in the other (slightly spilling). To the right of me with his back to me is the silver fox wearing a Sinatra hat, tilting it down with his hand, with a fox's tail. To the left of me is Fancy Pants, side on, looking sexy, eating from a plate of Tiramisu. Then, Mr Belfast is lying on the floor on his front, looking hot, and hairy, holding a bunch of shamrocks. My heel is on top of him, pinning him down, under a pile of three books. The background is spotlights on all of us." I beamed enthusiastically at him."What do you think?"

"It's a very visual image, but I'm not sure its sophisticated enough?""The artist has one heck of a job!" He smiled at me and shook his head."Is there no end to your talents, L.J.?" Taking his drink, he put the manuscript to one side."So, we've been talking for years now, but you've never really explained how all this came about. Why did you start writing? What was the motivation what were you like as a child?"

"Unrequited love, I guess, all throughout my life. And I got sick of not having a voice. When I write, I have one. So many people in my life stopped me from being who I really am. I had an awful childhood, which supressed me, a terrible marriage, which almost made me disappear, then I met this guy who just set me free. Sure enough, he broke my heart, but without meeting him and writing that first book, I'd have never tapped into this."

"So, Fancy Pants was some kind of trigger?" He rubbed his chin.

"I never thought of it that way, but yes, I guess he was—the rejection from him. Writing's my go-to for calm and relaxation, to escape. I suppose it's like an artist painting or a musician playing their instrument. It's my safe place. I think I'm more in love with writing than all three of the guys in the books put together." I sniggered into my drink.

"L.J., you do realise that these books at some point could go big, and you could potentially be famous? Mainly, I think, because it's a true story, and people will love the fact that there's an actual person behind them." He looked at me concerned, as he knew the content of what I'd written would leave me wide open to abuse."Fiction is easy to deal with, but real life… you'll have haters."

"Everyone has haters, most people judge others—hell... I've already had some pretty nasty reviews. If people want to feel that way about me, it's on them, not me. I've been going through a process writing these books. I think it will help more people than make them mad or upset." I looked to him for encouragement."God, everyone on the planet has sex! They like to learn about it and read about it. It's part of human nature."

"Not everyone wants to read about it, but I can see your point. So, it's about how you're going to handle yourself when all this does go viral and you're in the public eye. Once the manuscript's at its best, you need to find an agent, —UK or USA. I'd advise you to change publisher; choose one with a good reputation, or even set up your own publishing company?

"I've been married over 30 years. She's my best friend and we'll be together forever. She's my second wife. Whenever I think back about sex, I think of it being the one thing that always got me into trouble." He laughed at the memories of his past."Sex makes us make bad decisions," he said boldly."I must ask you, L.J., what's the big deal with Fox?" He's bad for you."From reading your work, I think you've a better chance with Mr Belfast than all the others in the book. He's made an effort to track you down. That's a big deal for a guy, you know?"

I put my burger down and felt a tug in my heart.

"Perhaps it's time to write about someone new? Write about love and sex when it's with the right person?" He tapped the tips of his fingers.

"I love FOX?" I put my hands in the air."It's always been him, bad or good for me, my heart made its decision a long time ago"!

"Well then go get your man, tell him how you feel", life way to short. I looked into his eyes and could see he had lost love once.

"I just need to finish this book so I can go back to having some kind of normal life. I've not stopped writing for one day in six years. It's been my priority—writing comes first. Sometimes, because I can't turn it off, it's felt like a curse. I even wake up in the middle of the night and start writing." It really has been taking over my life.

"I totally understand. I've experienced the same thing. Once you're a writer you'll always be a writer. I'm afraid this won't ever turn off. I used to go to writing groups to mix with likeminded people—perhaps you have some back in the UK?" He pointed to my notebook to write it down.

"Really, and explain I've written three filthy books to a group of other writers? They'll all want to try and shag me." I joked but was partly serious.

"I didn't think about that." He scratched his head."Maybe not then—for now," he chuckled quietly to himself."Have you had any formal training, done anything to help guide you in writing these books?"

"No, they just came to me, and I wrote them." He didn't seem surprised.

"Well, you certainly have the drive to do it, I have to say." He looked at me proudly."Right, we have the basics covered off. Make the first chapter and last chapter outstanding and find out where your middle is. And if you don't have one, think of something gripping and engaging—we need three waves of impact. Then I need you to go through every chapter and re-read it, make it more to the point. Don't ramble and give it your soul. Stop holding back. Do what you did with A Year of Tiramisu; include the passion and the drama; let the readers feel all your emotions." I was frantically taking notes while trying to make eye contact, so he knew I was listening.

"Consider re-writing 'A Year of Tiramisu.' It's not your best work. You're experienced now, so publish a 2nd edition. You could make that story a sensation."

"Maybe call it a year of Tiramisu two?" I suggested and he nodded in agreement.

"Now, turn the page, and let's discuss what you need to prepare for the film producers you'll approach." He waved his hand for the waiter and ordered some coffee. I listened to him and made notes, mesmerised by the information, the detail, and the enthusiasm he had to help me. I knew that from this day on, my life was going to change forever, and that I was exactly where I wanted to be. He'd confirmed it, I was a writer, and a thumping good one according to him.

"Quick question before we start rearguing casting. Would you offer to play L.J.? I mean, after all, it's your story—who better to act it out?" He searched me for a response.

"I would love to play the part of L.J.! But I'll need to slim back down a few stone perhaps and get some fake teeth.

"Have you thought about actors for the three men?"

"Christian Bale from American Psycho perhaps for the silver fox: an emotionally removed sexy psychopath with a surprising soft side. He has such a presence on screen and plays such a great bad guy. I can see him in a filthy movie, and we'd be on fire together."

"Mr Belfast—Gerard Butler. He's a sexy Scottish actor whom everyone loves, full of character and warmth, and he can do a mean Irish accent. He's fun and childlike; he'd be perfect." I'd get a serious crush and forget my lines working with him, for sure, I daydreamed.

"And Fancy Pants?" He cleared his throat.

"I think he should audition for himself too; be some great chemistry." I laughed into my drink.

He seemed stunned by the thought I'd put into this."Have you thought of a leading lady if they won't cast you?"

"I love Margot Robbie, and she's mad as a box of frogs like me. She has my attitude in her scenes with the Joker in Suicide Squad, f*cked up beyond repair at times, but deep down a total pussycat. But there's no way she'd do it, she'd have to go back to being brunette. I think they'd struggle to get anyone to act out the sex scenes." I was deadly serious."I'd play the part for free if it got a movie released."

"You've got everything figured out, haven't you?" He showed great respect.

"I've been living and breathing this for what seems forever. I have a vision. never doubted it would go somewhere, because no one has ever dared to write about their life this way before."

"You're a very brave woman. I really do wish you all the best." He reached over and shook my hand, smiling widely.

"Thank you. Now, what do I need to prepare for the film producers, tell me everything…" I could hear the chatter of people around me as I watched Mike's lips move as he spoke to me, and for a few seconds felt like I was somewhere else, in a dream. As I wrote my notes, I realised that it'd taken me to the exact age of forty-three to find my true calling in life. I loved who I was and had become; this was me. I was truly inspired and alive, and this was only the beginning of my journey.

It didn't matter who I was dating, how much amazing sex I did or didn't have, what the balance in my bank account was, or how many material things I had in my possession. It was all irrelevant. It was always about me, my soul and making myself happy by being who I was truly supposed to be. I was in control of me, and no one could take that from me or tell me how to live or how to be. I felt a sense of peace I'd never known before. I was falling in love with myself, and I couldn't wait for what was to happen next, I was going to write a screenplay, and make a movie. I couldn't wait to get back on the plane home to tell Fox everything, and more importantly to tell him how much I loved him and that I was certain of it.

CHAPTER TWENTY-NINE

"Everything I do" ~ Bryan Adams

Arriving at Manchester Airport, I stepped off the plane, feeling the rush of cold air hit my face as I took a deep breath. This was home, yet it felt foreign, as though everything around me had shifted subtly in my absence. The hum of the terminal, the familiar British accents, even the smell of rain on the tarmac—they all brought a sense of bittersweet nostalgia. I was finally back, but my heart and mind had changed profoundly.

My thoughts were consumed by the idea of seeing Fox. The longing to share my journey and the lessons I had learned burned inside me. I had made up my mind to write a screenplay inspired by our love story, and I was eager to tell him. Jet-lagged but exhilarated, I found my car and punched his office address into the satnav. As the car roared to life, I put on my sunglasses, cranked up the music, and rolled down the windows, letting the wind whip through my hair as I sang along.

For the first time in my life, a sense of peace settled over me. I was genuinely happy, in love, and ready to embrace whatever the future held. The drive took nearly two hours, each mile filled with anticipation. Finally, I pulled into his work's car park and scanned for his car, and I found it. I touched up my make-up, sprayed on a bit of perfume, and flashed a wide smile at my reflection. My heart pounded with excitement.

The rain began to fall as I dashed across the car park, the cool droplets mingling with my excitement. I pushed through the revolving doors into the company's lobby, approaching the receptionist with a confident smile.

"Hi, I don't have an appointment, but I'm here to see Fox. Could you let him know I'm here?" I asked, my voice steady despite the fluttering in my stomach.

She gave me a curious glance before picking up the phone."Fox, I have a Miss Brown in reception. She doesn't have an appointment. Would you be able to see her?" After a pause, she put down the phone."He said he's got back-to-back meetings all day but can spare a few minutes. He's on the 5th floor, second door on the right." I will take you there.

I thanked her and we headed for the lift, my heart racing with each step. As directed, I walked down the hallway to his office, the anticipation grew, my mind racing with thoughts of what I would say, how I would feel seeing him again. This man meant everything to me. He was the one I wanted to marry, the love of my life. I knocked softly on his door, and his voice called out for me to enter.

His office was immaculate, a small space lined with business books but no windows. He stood as I entered, his eyes locking onto mine, a familiar heat passing between us.
"L.J., what are you doing here? You know I don't like surprises," he said, a mix of disbelief and concern in his voice as he crossed the room to embrace me.

"I got off the flight from Alabama a few hours ago," I explained, my voice quivering with emotion."I drove straight here because I couldn't wait another second to see you. I missed you so much, and I'm sorry for everything—for acting like a child when you've been through so much."

His eyes softened as he brushed a stray hair from my face."I missed you too, you crazy girl. How did it go? What did he think of your work?"

I grinned, feeling my heart swell."He loved it! He said it's definitely movie material. I need to learn how to write a screenplay, and he's got some contacts in New York. That's the next step: writing the screenplay based on book three and then presenting it to movie producers."

His eyes widened."I told you you could do it. You're going to be a big star. You deserve to be. You're brilliant. It's the natural progression."

I touched his face, feeling the warmth of his skin under my fingertips."I couldn't have done any of it if I wasn't in love with you," I whispered, and we fell into a passionate kiss."I love you so much, Fox. I will never love another."

He held my gaze for a moment, his eyes revealing a depth of feeling that words couldn't capture. But then he let go, stepping back toward his desk.

"I have meetings, but you're not driving back to Yorkshire. You're too tired, and I don't want you to cause an accident. Here's my room key," he said, scribbling down an address."Go get some rest, and we'll have dinner tonight. There's something important I need to talk to you about."

I nodded, exhaustion creeping in."You're probably right. I don't know how I'm functioning right now," I admitted, a mix of excitement and weariness in my voice.

"It's five minutes away. Go grab a shower, get into a robe, and I'll see you later," he smiled, turning back to his computer.

Just then, there was a knock at the door and the receptionist's voice carried through the room:"Fox, I'm sorry to interrupt your meeting, your phone must be on silent, your wife's called. It's a family emergency." She was out of breath from running from the lift.

The words hung in the air like a death knell. He looked at me, his face ashen with shock. My heart shattered into a million pieces as the realization hit me. His betrayal and dishonesty washed over me, my lip quivering as I backed toward the door, the receptionist now looking and feeling very uncomfortable.

"Not you, Fox. Not you," I whispered, my voice breaking.

"L.J., it's not what you think it is!" he shouted after me, but it was too late. I had already turned and fled, the pain cutting deeper with each step until I left the building and got into my car.

Back to The New York Times.

The room was thick with silence. The city outside was darkening, the lights flickering to life and casting a magical glow over the streets. I stared out the window, the weight of my story pressing down on me.

The reporter had stopped writing, his expression one of stunned disbelief."So, he'd been married all along? That makes perfect sense now, why he didn't want to commit and was acting so oddly. But you deeply loved him?" He looked perplexed, scratching his head.

"Yes, I did, and I still do, even after what I found out. Love doesn't just go away, it stays with you forever, even if it's a deep wound and profound sadness; that's how I knew it was true love for me." Regrettably, I went back and forth for what seemed forever, expecting him to leave her and be with me; that day never came. Everything I did, I did it for him; I would have moved mountains. Even after I knew, I would have died for him; I loved him that much. I just wanted to understand him, but he never let me in.

The last time we spoke was over a video call, and it ended with him seeing me cry. He said he wasn't my future, and that he would never be my husband. The reality of the situation couldn't have been clearer; I was, and always had been, nothing to him other than fun."

It's taken time to heal, and a big leap of faith, but I learned the most important lesson of my life; after heartbreak, I learned how to love myself. He was a lesson I had to experience to get to where I am now.

I bit my lip and blew my hair away from my face."Life can be unpredictable, but we learn from pain, we learn from mistakes, and it can all be turned into a positive!"

"You're so strong L.J, what did you do next?" he asked, his voice softened.

"I wasn't so strong at first. I fell completely apart. I nearly drank myself to death; I used it to cope. It became a real problem. I put on a lot of weight. I couldn't look in the mirror. I hated myself. I felt like I wasn't good enough. I felt so much guilt, so much shame, and I couldn't believe how stupid I'd been to miss the signs; they were all there, I just couldn't see them, or I simply had refused to. It almost destroyed me. I went down a deep rabbit hole that consumed me. I thought if I died, no one would ever notice or even care. In my head, I was nothing to anyone, I actually hoped before I went to bed at night that I wouldn't wake up again."

"Then, I woke up one day and it all just stopped! I'd stopped self-sabotaging. Slowly, I stopped drinking, and I got back on my feet and started to look after myself again. It was a slow process, a long hard one, but I got there. I thought to myself, no one can look after me apart from me, so I better make sure I have the best in life.

I took the advice of my editor in Alabama." I continued, my voice steady despite the storm of emotions."I channelled all the pain, all the loss, all the hate, all the anger and sadness, into a screenplay. I have a meeting here in New York tomorrow to talk about turning it into a movie. I wasn't going to lose my writing; I'd lost enough in my life, it's all I had and all I knew, I guess you could call it my purpose in life!"

"So, you see, this isn't just a story about a woman writing about relationships and sex," I continued, a passionate fire igniting in my eyes."It's the story of how I fought to become Liberty Jane—a journey from author to screenplay writer—from a broken woman to an empowered goddess. Despite my life being filled with so many unfortunate events, twists, and turns, I produced one hell of a story, and I overcame everything! If I have to knock on every film producer's door in America to get this on the big screen, I will!" This will be my karma, something good has to come out of all this pain.

The reporter looked at me, admiration in his eyes."It is going to make one hell of an exclusive, that's for sure!" He clapped his hands together.

"It's not that I'm so smart, it's just that I stay with problems longer," I quoted Albert Einstein, a smile tugging at my lips.

He chuckled, closing his notebook and stopping the recording. "Do you want to grab a beer?" he asked, checking his watch. We were both emotionally exhausted from my storytelling.

"Sure, why not," I shrugged, picking up my bag. "I could do with a drink after spilling out my soul." I winked and gave out a sigh.

As the elevator descended, I caught a glimpse of our reflections in the polished metal walls. We stood in comfortable silence, each floor dinging softly, bringing us closer to the vibrant chaos of the streets below. The interview had been intense, a whirlwind of questions and revelations that left me both exhilarated and drained.

When we finally stepped out into the cool night air, he turned to me, a grin spreading across his face. "Well, L.J., that was some eye-opener of an interview!" His thick British accent carried a playful note, lightening the intensity that had enveloped us.

I couldn't help but laugh. "Oi, mister, be very careful mocking me about being British! We have J.K. Rowling, after all," I teased, giving him a gentle nudge with my elbow. The banter was a welcome relief from the formalities of our earlier conversation.

"Well, I think she might have some competition." His eyes sparkled as he winked back at me. We fell into an easy, flowing conversation as we walked out of the building. The city was alive, lights twinkling like stars brought down to earth, and the warm night seemed to wrap around us, making the world feel infinite.

We stepped into an Irish bar just across the street, the warm glow of the dim lights casting a welcoming spell. I caught the bartender's attention with a smile. "Two pints of Guinness, please." As I reached for my credit card, Adam insisted on paying, his gesture as chivalrous as ever.

A man standing across from us at the bar looked over, his eyes twinkling with curiosity. "I love your accent," he called out, his voice carrying charm. He picked up his pint and began to make his way over to us. "What part are you from? I love your voice," he continued, his enthusiasm infectious.

"The beautiful Yorkshire Dales," I replied, smiling warmly, slightly taken aback by his forwardness. "Where are you from?"

"L.A. Just here for a writer's convention," he said, his words weaving a sense of adventure.

"Wow, that's amazing. I'm a writer too. Oh, this is Adam," I introduced. "He's a reporter from the New York Times." We received our drinks and started looking for a seat, the pints brimming with promise.

"What's your name? Do I know your work?" he asked, not giving me a moment's peace, his eyes sparkling with excitement.

"Liberty Jane Brown, but everyone calls me L.J.," I said, extending my hand. He took it with a gentle, yet firm grip.

"Jamie," he said, "ex-boxer, aspiring writer. It's new." He shrugged his shoulders and beamed at me, his smile radiating a sense of newfound purpose.

Adam nudged me, causing a few drops of my drink to spill. He whispered in my ear, "Like in the tarot card reader's prediction!" I looked at Jamie, momentarily stunned, as the memory of the mystical reading flashed in my mind like a forgotten dream.

"Are you okay, L.J.?" Jamie asked, concern softening his features."Here, let me carry that for you."

"Do you mind if I sit with you guys?" he asked, his voice laced with an almost otherworldly kindness.

"Liberty, this is pure magic," Adam winked at me and drank some of his pint, then we all sat down together.

"I didn't even need to use a magic wand," I smiled into my pint."

"Am I missing something?" Jamie asked trying to figure out what our conversation was about."

"We were just discussing the magic of serendipity," I beamed at him."Tell me all about your ideas."

THE END

Other published work

A year of Tiramisu 2018
A year of SINatra 2020

Printed in Great Britain
by Amazon